9,74

THE UNBEATEN

Giles A. Lutz

THE UNBEATEN

DOUBLEDAY & COMPANY, INC.
GARDEN CITY, NEW YORK   1972

THE UNBEATEN

CHAPTER ONE

Matt Norborne paced back and forth, his agitation showing in his restlessness. He was a big man with a long, vigorous stride, and something drove him. Every now and then he smashed a fist into a palm. Where in the hell was that wagon? It was almost a day late and the Chinese crew of pipelayers were sitting on their haunches, eating up Matt's wages. They couldn't be blamed for the wagon not being here, but that didn't help the drain on Matt's dwindling capital.

"How deep you figure on wearing that path?" Riley Duncan asked and grinned. Duncan was an older and smaller man than Matt. He was good-humored until he was crossed and it took a lot to get him aroused. When he was, he was as dangerous as a wounded grizzly. A newcomer would be startled at the first sight of him. At a distance the left side of his face looked a permanent blue. Anybody who had been around miners long enough was familiar with that discoloration. It was the trademark of an old powder man. If he handled powder long and often enough, the chance of one of those shots going wrong was almost inevitable. If that powder man was lucky enough to live through a premature blast, the grains of powder driven into his skin would give it that odd pigmentation.

Matt smashed his palm again. "Where is that goddamned wagon?"

Duncan didn't bristle at the tone. He knew the question wasn't directed at him. He pulled the battered pipe out of a face that was framed by a ring of thick, wiry beard and spat on the ground. He contemplated the moist spot. "As short as water is in this country, Matt, it seems a shame for a man to have to waste his water that way."

1

That nearly pulled a grin out of Matt. He knew Duncan was trying to talk him into an easier mood, but when money was running short, a man couldn't help but be worried.

The grin didn't quite come off. "When that driver gets here, I'm going to hang him up by his queue."

Duncan jerked his head toward several men, squatting in whatever sparse shade they could find. "Better hadn't let them hear that. They're clannish."

Matt acknowledged that with a rueful nod. The chatter of the Chinese carried faintly to him. They were confirmed gamblers, and they were back at it again. Fantan was the only game he had seen them play. He knew its rudiments, but the game carried no appeal to him. Players bet on a single number from one to four, and the banker counted off a large handful of beans or pebbles in fours from a bowl. If a player guessed the remaining number in the banker's hand, he won. It fascinated the Chinese. Matt had seen them so absorbed in it, that no outside word got through to them.

He listened to their talk and shook his head. It seemed he would never understand their tongue, and he was completely helpless when it came to their writing. It was a good thing that Lo Yen had some English at his command. Through him Matt delivered his orders. Most of them were small, wiry men with unblinking eyes in an inscrutable face. Matt hadn't the slightest idea of what they thought of him, nor did it concern him too much. They worked for half what it would take to hire a white man. They were willing workers, and he could swear they could outlast a white man, particularly on a repetitious, monotonous job. He had believed in their reliability until the wagon had been overdue for so long. One of the Chinese had driven it to the railhead, and two more had gone along to help him load the pipe.

Duncan had been watching the fantan game, and he said with mild humor, "Maybe they've stopped to play that damned game."

Matt swore. To him, it had no humor at all. He scowled

2

at the hazy horizon, hoping to see a dust cloud that denoted movement under it. He saw nothing more encouraging than the other times he had looked in that direction.

"Maybe I should have hired white drivers," he fretted. Duncan shook his head. "None of them would work with us since you hired all Chinks."

That was the common slang name for them, and it irritated Matt. "Don't you like them, Riley?"

The reflection of Matt's irritation showed in Duncan's shrug. "Hell, how do I know? I can't even get to know one of them. Get close, and they shut up. Even if a man could learn their jabbering, how will he ever get to know them?" He frowned at them. "Every now and then I get the feeling they're giving us a going over."

That did bring a laugh from Matt. "You can bet on it. Just like we're talking about them now. We're as strange to them as they are to us. You can be thankful for one thing. They've laid a lot of pipe for what we've paid them. They made our money stretch a hell of a long way farther."

"I ain't unhappy about them, Matt. You're the one who's talking about hanging one of them by his queue."

"Oh hell." Matt threw up his hands. "The way you can twist things around."

There was a strong bond between these two, even though their natures clashed at times. They had thrown in together before they left Comstock and had continued the association after they came to Candelaria, Nevada. Between them they got an astonishing amount of work done, though they went at it in different ways. Matt was the hard driver, plowing determinedly into anything that blocked his path. Duncan accepted things more placidly, doing what he could about it and shrugging off what he couldn't handle. Several times, his mild acceptance had driven Matt wild. It had been the cause of their few heated arguments, and afterward, Matt had been relieved it hadn't deteriorated into fists. His size said he could whip Duncan, but he knew he would pay a sizable

3

bill in physical battering. No argument was worth the fragmenting of the bond between them.

He was a tall, angular man, halfway through his twenties. He had handled a lot of hard rock in his last five years, and it showed in his arms and shoulders. He wasn't a handsome man, but the trim bulk of him could arrest a lot of female eyes. His nose was too prominent for good looks, but his mouth was cut on generous lines cut for ready laughter. His eyes were the shade of slate that could warm with his mood, or freeze with equal rapidity. His nature was like an April day; storming one moment and smiling the next. His hands were hard and callused, and his clothing showed the effect of long and rough wear. He rarely thought about how he looked. He had more on his mind than to worry about his appearance.

Duncan was taking this new setback with a too happy-go-lucky mood. "Don't you realize what will happen if we run out of money?" Matt stormed.

That didn't sober Duncan. "I've been there before. It can happen again."

"You accept it," Matt half-shouted. "Goddamn it! I won't."

He was wrong about the Chinese being completely absorbed in their game, for his outburst turned heads his way. He wasn't apologizing to Duncan or to them for it. He had a dream, and it wasn't as wild as it had first sounded. He was going to bring water into Candelaria, and the pipeline was half-laid. This was the kind of a dream that could make a man wealthy. Sure, there was self-service in it, but it would give a lot of service to the public, too. Water cost a dollar a gallon in Candelaria and was freighted in from the Trail Canyon in the White Mountains. Sikeston had been hauling water out of that spring until Matt had filed a claim on it. Sikeston had made a lot of threats, but he had moved on a little farther. Matt had kept an eye open for him, but so far he had had no trouble from the man.

He had been working a silver mine with Duncan when the dream hit him in the middle of the night. It had jolted him

4

upright, and for a long moment, he couldn't separate the real from the imagined. It had been under his nose all the time, and he hadn't been able to see it. What was the most luxurious thing in this country? Water! Give the people that luxury at a price they could afford, and a man could make a fortune. He had just been looking in the wrong place for that fortune.

He had shaken Duncan awake, and his words had poured forth. Duncan had listened to him, squinting his eyes. He didn't respond immediately to Matt's plan for he said, "You weren't drunk when you went to sleep, but I guess you got hold of it somehow."

Matt's eyes had been blazing with the vision he saw. "Just shut up and listen to me."

At first Duncan kept shaking his head, but that had lessened as his eyes grew rounder. He was a slow thinker, and the best he could give Matt right at the start was, "Matt, I dunno. Nine miles is a hell of a long way. Where will we get nine miles of pipe?"

Matt had all that thought out. "Out of San Francisco." He waved aside Duncan's objection. He knew how far away San Francisco was. "We can ship by the Central Pacific, then transfer to the Carson & Colorado Railroad."

Duncan thought he had a point there, and he jumped on it triumphantly. "The Carson Colorado ain't built here yet. It's only built to Belleville."

"I know where they are," Matt said impatiently. "We can freight by wagon from Belleville to Candelaria." As the crow flies that was twenty miles. It was rugged country, and the road twisted and turned through it. It was considerably longer the way a wagon had to travel, but a wagon could get through it.

"But the railroad's going to build to Candelaria," Duncan said. "Why don't we just wait until we can ship by rail all the way?"

"And have somebody think of this and jump it right under our noses. Hell no! We don't sit around and wait."

5

Matt had crashed through every obstacle Duncan had thrown up. "I know it will work. Listen—" The rest of that night had been lost as far as sleep was concerned.

He had proven it would work, or at least was working. Time and money were big, important details, but give a man an idea, and he pared away at the things that hampered it. All of his life he had known poverty, or at least the edge of it. Southern Missouri land had given no more generously than the rock and sand of Nevada, but the difference was that Nevada land had opportunities where there had been none in southern Missouri. Those Missouri hills were poor and thin, and it had killed his mother through unremitting overwork. It had furrowed his father's face and bent a once-straight frame. But a natural stubbornness had kept his father hanging on. Maybe losing his wife had killed the spirit in him. Maybe he had died with her going, leaving only the final laying down to do.

Matt's father's face had faded away until it was hazy in his memory, but he could still remember his words. Next year would be better, his father had promised. Next year would bring the rain they needed at the right time. Next year we'll get the crops planted when they should be. His father couldn't have really believed those words. The parade of the long years had proven them to be monstrous lies. Matt guessed that the habit of repetition had seized his father until he couldn't see things the way they actually were. The old man had died still saying it. "Don't ever sell the land, son. Hang onto it. Don't—"

Matt had covered his father's face with the blanket. The old man had lived a lie so long that he had died still trying to say it.

That land had been a cruel adversary. It had drained Matt's father until only a husk remained, a husk without inner strength to sustain it. Matt had known no racking grief. Maybe the end had been too long in coming until only a weary resignation remained.

He couldn't sell the land fast enough, and he felt no

6

sense of guilt as he had signed the papers. It would finally do something for a Norborne; it would give him enough money to make a fresh start someplace else. But after he paid up the outstanding bills, there hadn't been much left, only enough to get as far away as he could from that hostile land. For a long time he had thought that he had only changed one hostile land for another. Had he inherited his father's stubborn streak without the ability to see it? But he had hung on with that same dogged determination. All around him men had hit it rich. It would happen to him as long as he believed. All he had to do was to hang on another day, turn over another shovelful. But an idea was clamoring for acceptance. Hard work and determination were prime ingredients, but they weren't enough. A man needed a large element of luck and a fresh approach, an approach that the blindness of the masses wouldn't let them see.

He stared again in the direction from which the wagon should come. He was well aware of how short their money was growing and the distance of the pipeline left to be built. He and Duncan had sold everything they could get their hands on to scrape up every possible dollar. He had seen the silver claim go without much of a qualm, knowing that they would never make much more out of it than living expenses. He knew they had gone into this on the most fragile of shoestrings, and too many times he had felt he was at bay, ringed about by hungry wolves. He gave that picture as little room as he could, but it had lodged in his mind with a devil's persistence.

He had a funny feeling now that he couldn't dig out. The wagon wasn't coming; something had happened.

He wanted his face to be as inscrutable as the Chinese as he said, "Riley, I think I'll ride out and meet the wagon."

The loss of it wouldn't wreck him, but my God, how it would bend him.

Duncan heaved himself to his feet with a sigh. "I thought something like that was in your mind." He squinted at the

7

sun. It was beginning its long, downward slide. "We sure as hell ain't going to get to Belleville tonight."

"I don't figure on riding that far," Matt said irritably.

"We might have to. Maybe that pipe never got on the Carson Colorado. They sure need a lot of their supplies for their own building." There was that fatalistic shrug that at times drove Matt wild.

"Then we're going to raise a little hell," Matt snapped. "I paid for that shipment to get to Belleville."

CHAPTER TWO

Surely this land had to be of the devil's making, for God would never look upon it and call it good. This part of Nevada was a land of extremes, both of them bad. What wasn't desert was jagged mountains. Very little green grew in its sullen alkali flats or the blistering salt hollows. The harsher outlines of the mountains were just as bleak. Animal or bird life rarely ventured into it, for ordinary life couldn't survive here. This was the habitat of the lizard, the horned toad, and the rattlesnake. In some ancient time the boiling cauldron that was the earth spewed up the broken-backed ridges of the Excelsior Range and the barren crests of the Monte Cristos.

Matt looked at them with a jaundiced eye. He didn't relish even a horseback ride through them.

"I want to talk to Lo Yen, Riley. Will you saddle the horses?"

"Sure, Matt."

Matt looked back after a half-dozen strides, and Duncan still watched him. Duncan's face mirrored the anxiety Matt felt.

Lo Yen saw him coming and straightened. He must have being doing all right in the game. His pile of silver coins was higher than the other players'. He scooped them up and dropped them into a pocket of his black cotton pants. The light, buttoned coat was of the same material, and those odd-looking shoes didn't seem capable of lasting long in this rocky country. Either they had a durability that didn't show, or they were replaced frequently.

"Yes, boss," Lo Yen said. He still had the singsong quality in his voice, but his accent wasn't as bad as Matt had heard

9

in other Chinese. At least, he could understand Lo Yen. It struck him with odd force that he knew nothing about this man's personal life. He didn't know where Lo Yen lived, or if he had a wife or family. A man could work hour after hour with another and still not know a thing about him. He brushed aside the speculation. He had more demanding thoughts on his mind.

"Lo Yen, I'm going to ride out and meet the pipe wagon."

"You think trouble."

Was that an anxious note in Lo Yen's voice. Matt brushed it aside. "Damnit, no!" Why did everybody jump to conclusions.

The harshness of his reply didn't put even a ripple in the smooth mask of Lo Yen's face.

Matt softened his voice. "Something just happened to hold up the wagon. I'm going out to hurry it along. Keep the men in camp until I get back."

He thought morosely, they'll be here. Nothing could pull them from their game. The thought of how much it was costing him for them to play that game put a sick hollow into his stomach.

"I don't know when I'll get back."

Lo Yen nodded his understanding. One of the workers jabbered a question at him, and Lo Yen answered it in his native tongue.

Matt waited a moment, and his irritation grew. Lo Yen had no intention of interpreting that. He moved away, his irritation growing. That talking was about him. He didn't regret hiring the Chinese, but he wished he could understand them.

Duncan had the horses ready, and he handed Matt one of the big canteens. It should be more than enough, but Matt didn't know how far it would have to be stretched. In the early spring he had marked a couple of springs along this road, but their flow had been weak even then. He hadn't been back since, and he doubted those springs could have enough strength to run against the summer's hot weather.

10

Matt hooked the canteen over the saddle horn and mounted. He lifted the reins and nodded to Duncan. He had an urgency prodding him, but he kept the horses to a slow walk. The land began its upward tilt shortly after they started. The slope of a mountain reached out a long way before it made its harsh demands. That was a rugged peak ahead of them, reaching nearly ten thousand feet in elevation. It had no trees, and the stunted vegetation could only put out a sorry shade. The sun would beat fiercely on a man all the way to the top.

A crude wagon road twisted and turned its torturous course upward. A horse and rider had ample room, but on some of those hairpin curves a wagon's outside wheels would be sickeningly near the edge. Below the edge of the road there was nothing, and a man avoided looking over the edge to keep that queasy feeling out of his stomach.

Duncan was hunched over, his hat pulled low to shade his face. He was a hard-sweating man, and the discolored line on the crown of his hat was a good two inches above the band.

"Goddamn country," he muttered. "A man's a damned fool to buck it."

Matt put a sharp look on him. Was Duncan losing his usual optimism and humor? "Don't you think we'll get it built, Riley?"

Duncan managed a rueful grin. "I do. But I'm hot and sticky. A man gets uncomfortable, and he magnifies everything out of size. Matt, I'm worried about that wagon, too."

Matt nodded. Duncan spoke for both of them. What the two of them needed was to see the wagon coming down the road.

They stopped at the crest, and Matt stared along the road until it faded into the hazy distance. They exchanged looks without a word. What was there to talk about? They could see a long way, and the road was empty.

Matt lifted the reins. Maybe he had been hoping so hard that he had half-convinced himself that the wagon would be in sight. The rat teeth of anxiety had sharpened and was gnawing steadily away.

He let the horse pick its own way down the reverse of the climb. This side was as treacherous as the other, and a man didn't forget his caution. The only difference was that a man leaned a different direction in the saddle. Maybe he should have told Duncan to pack food. Maybe they would have to go all the way to Belleville before they learned a damned thing.

He hated these outside curves where the road seemed to hang over nothing. The sheer precipice at its edge seemed to drop endlessly, and if a horse went over the edge, nothing would stop it until it reached the bottom.

He kept his horse against the inside of the curve, his eyes fixed on the road. He didn't want the animal stepping into a hole or stumbling over a rock. The danger from either was probably exaggerated, but still, a man didn't get careless with mountain turns like this one.

He saw something on the outer edge of the road, a crumbling that looked fairly fresh. It could have been a natural caving, or a weight resting on that edge had broken it off. Wheels, getting too close to the edge, might have chewed away the outer lip of the road before it went over.

He swung down and handed his reins to Duncan. "Hold him, Riley."

"What is it, Matt?"

Matt shook his head. He didn't know yet, but some premonition had kicked away the support for his stomach.

He didn't see wagon tracks, but that didn't tell him anything. This was rocky soil, and the wind blew constantly. It could have wiped away the faint impressions wheels might have left.

He veered a few feet from that crumbled spot. Once it had started, more of it could give away under new weight. He peered over the edge, praying that he would not see what he now feared. He scanned the slope, beginning a few yards from the road. His eyes kept moving down the drop. A

12

wagon and horses going over here would not lodge against anything for quite a way down.

He saw something wedged between two rocks, and the black coloring of it stood out sharply on the slope. The lighter spots made in the more solid color could be human flesh.

He stared for a long moment to confirm his first impression. If that was a human figure, it didn't move.

He moved back from the edge, and Duncan was anxiously watching him. He repeated his first question. "What is it, Matt?"

"I think I've found the wagon."

Duncan blew out a gusty breath. "No," he said in violent disagreement. "You're seeing wrong."

"I wish I was," Matt said heavily. Duncan started to swing down, and Matt said, "Not here."

He took his horse's reins and led it back to a straight stretch of the road. He tested a bush, and its roots were stubborn, for he couldn't budge it. It was strong enough to anchor his horse, and he tied its reins, testing the knot a couple of times before he was satisfied.

Duncan was full of questions, but he waited until his horse was tied next to Matt's. "You saw the wagon?"

"No. But I think I saw one of the men. The wagon will be below him."

He led Duncan back to the spot and pointed out the figure to Duncan. Duncan stared for so long that it aroused a faint hope in Matt that he could be wrong.

"It's one of them," Duncan said dully.

"I'm going down, Riley." The figure was a good five hundred feet below them, and he didn't know how far it would take before he found the others and the wagon. There wasn't a chance that any of those men were alive, but he had to see.

"Both of us, Matt."

Matt shrugged. Nobody argued with that tone in Duncan's voice.

He slung his canteen around his neck, and as Duncan

reached for the other he said, "One should be enough." If it wasn't, then they'd run short.

He moved back along the road some fifty yards, and this looked like an easier way to descend. Easier only meant a degree; there were no easy ways.

They moved slowly downward, testing each hold or the solidity of a rock before they rested weight upon it. The canteen was a cumbersome thing, but Matt didn't mind it. He would be damned glad he had it long before this descent was finished. Before he had covered a hundred yards his shirt was sticking to his sweat-soaked back, and sweat kept running into his eyes, putting a burning into them.

He stopped for a brief rest when he found a spot large and level enough for both of them to stand on. He was aware of the demand he had put on his muscles. His legs were trembling, and his breathing came with more effort.

He guided Duncan's foot to the spot beside him.

He uncapped the canteen and offered it to Duncan.

Duncan spat out white cotton before he spoke. "Go ahead."

Matt tilted up the canteen and his throat worked several times. The water was tepid and metallic tasting.

He handed the canteen to Duncan. "This will make a man forget there's such a thing as cold water left in the world."

Duncan sloshed water around in his mouth before he spat it out. "Almost enough to make a man swear off of drinking."

Matt noticed the long tear in the knee of his pants. He had scraped the skin beneath the tear, and he could feel its stinging and see the slow ooze of blood. He couldn't do much about it now.

"Ready?" he asked as Duncan lowered the canteen.

Duncan wiped his mouth with the back of his hand. "As ready as I'll ever be."

Matt glanced down, corrected his course, and started his descent again. He had no doubt that was a man's body, lying between those two rocks. All the way down here he had been hoping he hadn't seen right.

They stood over Kung, and it wasn't a pleasant sight.

14

A human body couldn't take the merciless battering this one had taken without its gory evidence. The flesh was beaten into bloody pulp, and Matt doubted if any bones were unbroken.

Kung wasn't near the wagon, and Matt pondered over it. Kung must have dived from the seat just as soon as or shortly after the wagon had gone over. It hadn't saved him a thing.

Matt was suddenly furiously angry, and there was nothing to vent it on. A man worked his heart out to accomplish what he wanted, and just when he got where he could believe it was all possible, something like this happened. He clamped his lips tight. He had better, if he didn't want to sound like a raving madman.

"You think Kung drove it, Matt?"

Matt gave him a curt nod. The other two had been sent along to help load the pipe at Belleville. Kung was proud of his status as a driver. He wouldn't give it up to either of the others.

He thought he knew what Duncan was thinking, and his angry eyes warned him not to say it, though he could agree with it. Kung hadn't proven himself the most capable driver in the world.

He could see the wagon now, several hundred feet below them. The wreckage didn't look much like a wagon. It was scattered over a sizable area, and what was left of it could only be used for firewood.

They found the two other men and the four horses just above the remains of the wagon. Human and animal bodies showed the same awesome battering. Both men were nearly stripped of their clothing, though harness still remained on two of the horses. Matt stared at them with brooding eyes. Nothing more would bother man or animal.

Lengths of pipe were scattered all over, and because it had been chained to keep the load from shifting, it had ridden well enough until the wagon was smashed to pieces. Some of

15

that pipe had even been bent, showing the mountain's impact on them.

Duncan asked a question that was bothering him. "Can we get the pipe back up to the road?"

Matt stared at the road above them. He would say it was a good thousand feet of climb to get back up to it.

"No!" The word was harsher than he intended it, but the full measure of the loss was just hitting him. It would take two men to carry a length of pipe, and they couldn't carry it and climb that cliff. If he had enough rope, he might be able to hoist it to the top. Where would he scrape up that much rope? If he could find it, it would cost a small fortune. No, he had to take his loss, whether or not he wanted to swallow it.

"Let's get back up," he said.

Duncan took a final look at the wreckage. "I wonder what happened? Kung was a good driver."

Matt wondered too. Speed wasn't involved for the heavily laden wagon had to be crawling slowly up the grade. The accident could have happened with a quickness that froze men's minds, rendering them helpless. But the wagon wouldn't go over all at once. The drop of the wheels from the solid roadbed would come as a jar, then the inner wheels of the wagon would rise high in the air. It would turn over and over as it started its drop. Were all three of them frozen to the seat. Wouldn't all of them have tried to make a desperate jump for safety?

He sighed. Maybe Kung had; his body was found up much higher. Evidently, the other two had ridden the wagon until it had broken up under them.

He let Duncan climb a few feet before he started to follow him. He squinted at the shadow that was beginning to creep up the mountainside. The descent had taken far more time than he thought it would; the sun was setting fast. He wanted to get back to the road at least by dusk.

CHAPTER THREE

Gary Holden stood at the window of his office in Columbus, staring out at the expanse of the white, desolate flat. It stretched until the horizon hid it, and a man couldn't look at it long, particularly at this time of the day, for it reflected back the sun rays in dazzling, blinding rays.

Holden turned his head to ease his watering eyes. Even though it caused temporary discomfort, he liked this view. He had seen something here that all of the fools had missed. He had been late for the original silver strike around Candelaria. But even if he had been in time, he would have sought some other way of making his living than by digging in the ground. He had seen too many men break their backs and eventually their health by trying to dig wealth out of the rocky earth. A few hit it rich, but the percentage was so small that a man was crazy to even think of bucking it.

He turned to the desk and took a cigar out of the humidor. He demanded the best out of life with the least physical exertion, and he was thoroughly satisfied with his progress.

He puffed until several small, fragrant clouds drifted to the ceiling. He let the fools dig for him, and they paid for whatever he wanted.

He pulled a watch out of a vest pocket, glanced at it, then put it back. He still had fifteen minutes before his meeting with Steiger.

He stopped at the window on the other side of the room and looked into Columbus's main street. He was proud of this town; he had earned the right to it. He had founded it and watched it grow from a parched spot on the earth to a booming town. It was across the ridge from Candelaria and five miles from it. Some people said it could never catch up

17

with Candelaria, but he had proven them wrong before. The same people said he was crazy to build his quartz mill at the edge of the ancient, dry lake bed. It was only additional proof of their lack of foresight. He admitted that the richest silver mines were near Candelaria, but Candelaria lacked two necessary things to a quartz mill; abundant salt required in the chlorination milling of silver ore and water. This site had unlimited salt in the lake bed, and a meager flow of water on the slope to the north gave him what he needed. The heavy rhythm of the stamps, beating the ore to a crushed, grainy powder, was a pleasant sound in his ears. His milling charge was sixty dollars a ton, plus an additional eight dollars for transportation by pack trains over the rugged, desert mountains. Only the richest of ore could pay such charges, but Candelaria mines had that. The mine owners were getting rich from that ore. Why shouldn't he? Maybe it was about time that he raise the charge again. His chuckle was amused as he thought of the squawks that would tear out of the owners. The squawking wouldn't change anything. He had the nearest mill, and those owners would have to pay for its convenience.

He picked up his hat and brushed its nap with the sleeve of his coat. It was the best money could buy, and it fitted his demand of life.

He placed the hat on his head and examined its jaunty angle in the small mirror on the wall. He adjusted the knot of his tie and nodded with satisfaction. He was a meticulous man even in the smallest of details, and he wouldn't deny that he was vain. Why shouldn't he be? He knew the imposing picture he made. He was aware of how female eyes lighted when they rested on him. He could have his pick of the available women in Candelaria and Columbus and probably quite a percentage of the so-called unavailable ones.

The thought tickled him, and he bared his teeth, showing an unflawed line of strong, white teeth. He was a massive man but surprisingly quick for all his bulk. He had a square jaw that could easily turn pugnacious, and it was backed up by the coldness of startling blue eyes. His nose had a long,

18

thin line, and he thought it gave his face an aristocratic look. He had never been bested by another man in a fight or a deal, and it wasn't quite enough. He had thought many times that he would have liked to have been born a hundred years ago when a powerful man's word wasn't even contested.

"You've got no complaint," he said and grinned at his reflection.

He glanced at his watch again. Steiger should be waiting for him by now. He checked the bills in his pocket and nodded. He had more than enough to pay Steiger. He tucked a .38 pistol into the waistline of his trousers, adjusted the skirts of his coat, and the small bulge of the gun scarcely showed. A .38 didn't have the shocking impact of a .45 but at close contact it did nicely.

He frowned at the knock on his door. He had no time to talk to anybody now.

"Come in," he snapped.

His frown increased as Lee Sadler stepped into the office. Sadler was an agitator, always telling the other workers that their working conditions were bad, or their pay wasn't enough. He was a short, husky man with heavy, clumsy-looking hands. He was Welsh or Flemish, or some other outlandish race. That was the trouble with this country. It was getting filled up with foreigners. A man couldn't walk the streets without running into Mexican, Indian, Chinese, Irish, or Welsh. If the Americans cleaned them out and started all over, the country would be a whole lot better off.

"What do you want?" he growled. Sadler had a standing with the other workers. He had a voice as powerful as a bull's, and people listened to him. Holden had thought several times of firing him. But it would arouse dissent from the other men, and the pleasure it would give Holden wasn't worth the trouble it would cause.

Sadler was really disturbed over something. If Holden let him get started, it would be hard to shut him off.

"I haven't got time to talk to you now," he said coldly. He noticed the blue-gray stain on Sadler's left cheek had

19

grown more pronounced. It was called by the medical term of argyria, and it was a hazard of working with silver ore. Its staining made an irreversible and permanent pigmentation of the skin. Holden had talked to Dr. Forsyth about it; not from any real interest, but from the fact that it was coming up more frequently. It was a normal result of the swallowing or inhalation of colloidal silver. Forsyth said that anybody handling silver dusts or other waste, including the condensed vapor and spray from smelting operations should be protected. The melting pots should be well ventilated. Daily bathing should be a must, particularly washing before eating, and he had suggested masks where ventilation didn't keep the air clean.

"Look at my face," Sadler said, a forefinger touching his cheek.

Holden's eyes grew colder. He had relayed Forsyth's information to Sadler to pass along to the other workers. What did Sadler expect him to do about it? It was a hazard of the job, and Sadler was paid for accepting it.

"I told you what had to be done about it," he said in clipped tones. "Apparently, you paid no attention."

Sadler was wild-eyed, and his chest heaved. "How can a man take a daily bath in this country? There's not enough water for a man to even wash his hands."

The leaders in Holden's neck grew rigid. "Are you blaming me for that?"

Sadler's hands were bunched, and he was in the grip of a helpless rage. "My girl won't look at me any more. Last night, she said she didn't want to see me again."

Holden's eyes filled with open contempt. He supposed men in Sadler's class did have trouble finding a suitable woman, even without this handicap. What else could Sadler expect? He had little training and no schooling. His limited ability would keep him in a certain class, and there were no ladders that he could use to climb out of it. If Sadler needed a woman that badly, he could go to Lily Marston's bordello.

20

The thought amused him, and he put it into words. "Try the girls at Lily's. They won't care how you look."

Sadler sucked in a ragged breath, and the gleam in his eyes was wilder. "On what you pay me?" he stormed. "I work ten hours a day to make a bare living. That's seven days a week. If I took Sunday off, I wouldn't make enough to live on the following week."

He was getting back into the old, wearying argument, and Holden cut him short. "You're getting the going wage. You can walk out any damned time you please."

Sadler stared at him with bitter, accusative eyes. "You'd like that, wouldn't you? You don't give a damn whether or not a man starves to death."

Holden had listened to all of this he wanted to, and he stood.

"No, you don't," Sadler shouted. "You'd like to walk out on me, wouldn't you? You're going to listen to me. You're going to pay me for this." He touched the disfiguration again.

Holden's cold amusement returned. The man talked like a fool. "How am I going to pay you for that?"

"I want a thousand dollars. It'll let me go someplace else. It'll give me a new start."

Holden's short burst of laughter held no mirth. Sadler had better worry about his head rather than his cheek. Holden could just see what would happen, if he was crazy enough to ever set a precedent like this. Some of the other men in the mill were showing this discoloration. If Sadler got what he asked for, the others would be pounding at his door before the following day was out.

"You're out of your head," he said contemptuously. He started to brush by Sadler, and the man seized his arm. Sadler's breathing was so labored it sounded almost like a sob. "I said you're going to listen to me."

"You never learn anything, do you, Sadler?" Holden asked. He buried his fist in Sadler's belly. Agonized color filled Sadler's face, and his cheeks puffed out as the explosive burst

21

ripped out of his mouth. His eyes bulged as he bent over to clasp the hurt belly.

His chin was wide open, and it was a temptation to slug it. But if that jaw was as hard as Sadler's head, Holden would risk breaking a bone in his hand. Sadler wasn't worth that.

Holden stepped aside and locked his hands together. He brought them down in a sweeping blow, and the more durable edges of his hands smashed into Sadler's neck. It drove his head down, pulling his body against the floor.

Sadler wasn't out, but his movements were feeble and uncoordinated as he tried to turn over.

Holden watched him struggle with cold pleasure. He should have done this weeks ago. He was tempted to drive a boot into Sadler's ribs, and it took restraint to hold it.

Sadler managed to turn over. He tried to lift his head, and the strength wasn't in him. His voice was barely more than a whisper. "You'll hear more about this."

Holden was about to lash out in fury over Sadler's threats, but he remembered where he was going tonight after his meeting with Steiger and checked himself. He couldn't appear at the Imlers' house disheveled and stained.

"You're fired, Sadler," he said in a frozen, brittle voice. "If I see you on the place—" He caught the rest of it and breathed hard. He never made threats; he only carried out their action.

Sadler couldn't talk well, but he could hear, and his eyes showed despair and hatred. "All right," he wheezed. "I promise you'll hear more from this."

Holden's face was a savage mask. He also was a man who allowed nobody to threaten him. "If you mean the rest of the bastards who listen to you, they're fired, too. Every damned man jack of them. As of right now the mill is closed."

Sadler stared at him with round, disbelieving eyes. "You can't mean that. What will you do—"

"You stupid bastard," Holden raged. "You let me worry about that."

CHAPTER FOUR

Old man Jennings's broad grin displayed toothless gums as he drove the buggy the length of the livery stable's runway, stopping the mare before Holden.

"She's a purty thing, Mr. Holden."

Nobody was sure of his age, and he wouldn't tell. But age was literally drying him up. His skin was ancient, cracked parchment, and the veins stood out blackly against it. He was little more than a walking skeleton, his bones held together by the wrinkled skin. One of these days a strong wind off of the desert would catch him and blow him away.

It wouldn't be much loss, Holden thought. Some men lived far beyond their worth, though he couldn't deny that Jennings was spry to hold a job as hostler at the stable. He couldn't make much, but then, Holden doubted that Jennings needed much to live on. Old age annoyed him. Every time he came in contact with it he was affronted.

"I ain't seen anything purtier," Jennings said.

Jennings meant the brand-new buggy with its glistening, black varnish and the red-leather seat and trimmings. Even Holly Imler hadn't seen it yet, and Holden had waited impatiently the weeks it had taken for its arrival. The waiting time for the necessities of life would be drastically shortened when the Carson & Colorado Railroad finally finished its narrow gauge track from Belleville to Candelaria. Holden didn't want it to happen. Candelaria was waiting for two things, the arrival of the railroad and the coming of the water. His lips curled. He could do little about one thing, but he could block Norborne's hare-brained idea of piping water into Candelaria. He could stop the threat that the pipeline might raise against him, or at least, delay it until he had a secure hold on the

Imler money. That thought brought a frown to his face. Holly Imler was a drop of mercury. When a man tried to pin her down with a thumb, she spurted out from beneath it in all directions. She was as high-spirited as this mare had been, but she had to be handled differently. A whip could beat a mare into submission. By God, he almost wished he could take a whip to Holly Imler.

"I dusted the buggy off real good," Jennings said ingratiatingly.

Holden nodded impatiently. It wouldn't really do any good, for a film of dust would be back on the vehicle before he reached Candelaria. This was typical of Jennings's tricks to fish for an extra coin or two. Holden pulled a coin out of his pocket and dropped it into that sly, outthrust claw. Jennings was typical of the leeches that infested life. He needn't think that this one small success would bring him another.

He climbed into the buggy, and the mare danced impatiently against Jennings's grip on her bridle.

"Let her go," Holden ordered. He looked back before he turned the corner. Jennings still stood there, his mouth agape, a mark of the grip of approaching senility. God, what did a man like that have to look forward to?

He drove out of town and set the mare to the hard pull that climbed the ridge between Candelaria and Columbus. His thoughts went back to Holly and her father. Dent Imler was a wise mine owner, and he could see change coming and make it work to his advantage. A couple of months ago he had changed to the sixteen-horse team to pull the huge, ore wagons pulled in tandem. The trains of pack mules were a laborious and expensive way to move ore, and Holden knew a deep envy for Imler. That change to the ore wagons was bound to increase Imler's profits. Should he increase his charge per ton to Imler for milling? He briefly debated it. Right now he had Imler in a bind. Imler could change to another mill, but there wasn't one for miles around. Imler would be slow to face that increased cost, at least, until the railroad came in. That would open up the country and give Imler a wide choice.

24

He reluctantly abandoned the thought of increasing his charge. He had one strong hold on Imler through his daughter, and he had better concentrate on that. He was never sure of what Dent Imler thought of him. The man's eyes were always veiled whenever he looked at Holden. He said a quick and vicious oath. It didn't matter what Imler thought of him. It was only important what Holly Imler thought of him. He was well aware of how she handled her father. Imler bent over backward to give his motherless daughter whatever she wanted.

His eyes were alert as he neared the crest. The road was wide enough for those ponderous ore wagons and a buggy to pass, but that was with the consideration that only normal drivers drove this road. But Imler had changed to Chinese drivers, and they seemed to go wild with a set of reins in their hands. Holden had too often seen these big wagons crash down the slope in a crazy, careening course with those monkey people perched high on the seat, yelling encouragement to the horses in that gibberish language that only another Chinese understood.

At the crest, he halted the mare a moment to let her blow. The road ahead of him was empty. He had given Steiger instructions to meet him at the bottom of this back slope, and he had set it up that way so no one would know he had contact with the man.

He put the mare in motion again, and his thoughts went back to the Chinese. He didn't blame Imler for hiring them; those yellow monkeys worked for half the wage paid to a white worker. Holden knew what he was going to do. His temper had forced him to yell a rash promise at Sadler, but he was glad now that he had been forced into it. He would have to close down the mill for a few days while he made the changeover, but he would more than make that up in the decreased payroll.

He let the mare pick her own pace on the downward slope, watching for some sight of Steiger. He was beginning to curse the man for being late when Steiger stepped out

25

from behind a small hummock that had given him some small shade.

Steiger was a squat, misshapen man with a gross appearance and manner. His hair was long and scraggly, his clothing filthy and worn, and it looked as though Steiger and his clothing hadn't touched water this year.

Holden stopped the buggy, and Steiger walked over to it. Holden saw Steiger's tethered animal, and his nose wrinkled in disgust as the smell of the man drifted to him. He could tolerate Steiger because he was a useful man to hire for an unusual job. Steiger lived from one job to another, and he was a competent and reasonable workman. It was whispered and rumored that Steiger was a killer, but nothing had ever been proven against him.

"I thought you'd never get here," Steiger complained. "This damned sun would melt a man. Why in the hell couldn't I have met you in Candelaria?"

Holden didn't explain nor apologize his being late. As for Steiger's question surely the man was smart enough to know that Holden couldn't afford to be seen with him.

"Did you stop that wagon?" he demanded.

Steiger's eyes gleamed at the memory of a recent pleasure. "Hell, that was no job at all. I shouldn't be charging you for getting rid of some of those Chinks."

"The wagon?" Holden said impatiently.

"Norborne's sure ain't gonna use that wagon again. When I plugged the driver he reared up and pulled the teams over the edge. I picked the kind of a spot you told me to."

Holden wasn't interested in the details, he just wanted to know if the job was a thorough one. "Did you check?" he asked impatiently. "Will Norborne suspect anything?"

Steiger slapped his thigh. "I checked. The way that mountain chewed up those Chinks nobody will ever guess how they died. Norborne won't use that wagon or anything in it."

His eyes picked up a crafty shine. "That stuff must be damned important to Norborne."

Holden acknowledged it with a curt nod. Steiger didn't need to know any more about it. This was the first of his moves against Norborne, and that smashed wagon had to hurt him badly. Holden would keep on hurting him until he abandoned the idea of bringing water into Candelaria. He had scoffed the first time he had heard about it, but he had kept an eye upon it. After Norborne had laid as much pipe as he had, Holden had to admit it was feasible. He didn't give a damn whether or not the town got water, but it could be a pressing matter to him. Plentiful water meant that a mill could be built at Candelaria. A wealthy man, such as Dent Imler, could do it, if it ever occurred to him. Norborne's pipeline could remove the one restriction against such a prospect. Holden wasn't going to stand by and see competition rise and grow.

"I may need you again," he said and reached for his money. It depended upon how hard Norborne discouraged.

He counted out ten bills and put the rest of it away. The agreed price was one hundred dollars down and a similiar amount after the job was done.

That crafty shine grew in Steiger's eyes. "Seeing as how important that job was to you maybe I didn't charge enough."

Holden felt the heat of blood rushing into his face, but he managed to keep his voice even. "This is the price we agreed on. I'll probably have more jobs for you." It was a subtle warning that Steiger was a damned fool to be so short-sighted.

Steiger shook his head. "I got this one done. Now I can see I done it too cheap."

Holden felt a throbbing band tighten around his head. "What did you have in mind?"

"Double the price should be about right," Steiger said. He watched Holden's face, trying to pick up some reaction. He thought he had a lever in his hand, and he tried to do a little prying with it. "Maybe Norborne might be interested in picking up some information."

27

Holden's rage almost choked him. This dirty bastard thought he had him, that he could dictate the new terms. Now he could see his error in picking this man, but when he had offered the two hundred dollars, Steiger had grabbed for it. He had thought him dependable, but now he saw the real danger in him. Steiger could go to Norborne, trying to play one off against the other.

"Norborne would break your neck, if he knew your part in this." Steiger laughed. "He don't have to know my part. I'd just tell him I know the man who was behind it."

Holden seemed lost in deep thought, then he nodded. "I see your point. It has value to you."

His face was blank against the seething turmoil within him. This vermin had to be stamped on, just as he would step on any insect.

"Then I owe you another two hundred dollars," he said and reached for the pocket where he had put the rest of the money.

Steiger watched with eager, avid eyes, his mind blank of anything else but the money.

Holden reached inside his coat, and his hand closed on the butt of the pistol. This animal didn't even sense potential danger to him.

He pulled out the pistol and aimed it at Steiger's head. "You damned fool," he said.

Steiger made a frantic clawing at his gun, and the alarm hadn't fully spread over his face when Holden shot him between the eyes.

The mare reared at the gunfire sound, and Holden was busy for a moment, controlling her.

"Easy, girl. Easy."

She steadied, but a trembling still rippled up her legs and into her body. Her ears twitched back and forward.

Holden looked dispassionately at the body. The damned fool didn't deserve the right to live.

He looked all about him, and the country was empty. Steiger was close to the road; he would be found soon. It didn't matter. This would only please most of the people. As for Holden being associated with him would never occur to most heads. A gentleman like Holden never soiled his fingers by touching something like Steiger.

Holden lifted the reins. "Let's go, Lady. We've got another lady waiting for us."

CHAPTER FIVE

Holly met him with outstretched hands at the door of her home. Holden drew her to him, and she fought it with a playful resistance. He bent his head and kissed her long, and his breathing was faster, his voice huskier as he raised his head.

"Damn, if you don't get more powerful each time."

The kiss had its effect on her, too, for he saw the rapid rise and fall of her bosom. "Gary, stop it."

"You know it, don't you, Holly? How long do you intend to keep a man waiting? How long do you think he can stand it?"

The crimson burned deeper in her face. He still didn't think of her as the most beautiful woman he had known, but she was attractive enough to flame the desire in him higher. He had paid little attention to her when he first saw her, but that had changed quick enough when he had learned who she was. A fortune behind a woman was the most potent beauty aid she would ever find.

Individually, each feature of her could be flawed, but blended together they made a picture that grew on a man. Her eyes were almond-shaped, and the shade of the green of them went well with her coppery hair. Her nose was patricianly formed, and judging by Imler's nose hers had to be an inheritance of her mother. She had a generous-sized mouth, but a smile or a laugh always softened it.

He bent his head, seeking her mouth again, and she evaded him. "Stop it, Gary. Before Dent comes out and sees us."

He gave her a speculative regard. "Are you ashamed of him seeing me kiss you?"

Her eyes danced with amusement. Gary's feelings were so

easily offended. "Of that kind of a kiss," she retorted. Her heart was just beginning to ease down its rapid beating. "I don't care about him seeing us. It's just that I am afraid of what I would do next."

He still held her hands, and he tried to draw her to him again. "What is it? Come on, tell me," he coaxed.

Her laughter was the happy tinkling of bells. "If you don't know, you'll learn. Think of the fun of waiting."

"I've already waited far too long," he grumbled, but he was smiling.

That made her eyes shine. She tucked her hand under his arm. "Dent is waiting for us in the parlor."

He wanted to hoot at her gullibility for believing what he said about waiting. He had rarely waited for anything in his life, and the need for a woman certainly wasn't one of them. At times, what he called her coyness irritated him. She belonged in that class of women that a man had to marry to get.

He walked into the parlor, and this room had always impressed him with its rich furnishings. The entire house was like that, for Imler had poured money into it. Holden didn't have the money to afford a home like this, but one of these days he would. Maybe he would eventually wind up owning this one. It was within the realm of probability. Dent Imler was in his upper fifties, and the hard, early years had marked him heavily. He had married late, and Holly was his only child. With the loss of his wife, he had turned more and more to his daughter. Holden suspected he would fight any man who tried to take her away from him. It might be an unconscious effort, but just the same he would make it.

Imler started to rise, and Holden said, "Don't get up, Dent. I'm here so often I don't feel I should have any special standing."

Imler grunted and sank back in his chair without offering to shake hands.

Holly flashed Holden an amused look that said, that's his way. He's a crusty old bear, but she said, "You know better than that, Gary. I'll see how near supper is."

31

Holden's eyes followed her out of the room. "An amazing woman," he said softly.

Imler grunted again, and it could have meant anything. His face was a granite crag, eroded by the years. He had hooded, gray eyes that always seemed to be judging a man, and Holden had noticed a smile rarely extended to them; particularly for him. Imler's arms were knotted with muscles from the early years of handling hard rock, and his blunt, stubby hands were still hard and gnarled. He was a weathered strip of rawhide, and at times, Holden was hard put to hide his annoyance with him. Imler wore clothes that were little better than the men he hired. He had long ago climbed out of the class of a laborer. Why didn't he show it? Holden gave him no credit for the rich furnishings of the house. That was Holly's taste and her doing.

Imler offered him a cigar, and Holden accepted it, though he didn't appreciate it. This was the cheapest of tobacco, and Holden's palate had been trained for something far better. Imler did indulge himself in one thing; good food. He had fresh meat hauled in frequently from Fish Valley, and his poultry and fruit came from as far away as Owens Valley in California. If a special viand wasn't on his table, it was because Imler couldn't find it within reaching distance.

Imler waved at a decanter of wine, and Holden declined it. Imler's tastes in wines were no better than his tastes in tobacco.

Holden wanted to talk about his trouble with Sadler, and he sought for a way to open the subject. He tried with a direct question. "Any trouble at the mine, Dent?"

Imler gave him a sharp glance. "Why should there be?"

Holden repressed his surge of irritation. Imler always answered a question with another one. He shrugged and said, "I had trouble at the mill, today."

He had Imler's interest, Imler's eyes showed it. "What kind of trouble?"

"Labor trouble. Sadler made another of his impossible demands."

Was that an appreciation in those cold gray eyes? Holden wasn't sure. "I won't have it any more. The man is always agitating."

"Try paying your men a little more than the going rate." Imler rotated the cigar in his lips as he lit it. "I pay fifty cents more a day."

Holden suppressed a gusty sigh. Imler always managed to work in a lecture. The man though he was God Almighty.

"I cut him down for good," Holden said. "I fired him."

"Ah," Imler murmured. "That could only bring you more trouble."

Before Holden could defend his action Holly appeared in the doorway. "Supper's on the table."

Holden's lips were thin with anger as he followed Imler into the dining room. He could have expected that Imler wouldn't agree with him.

He seated Holly, then sat down across from her. He had never seen a more beautiful roast, and it looked done to perfection. He thought of what it would bring downtown, even if one could find one like it.

Imler carved the roast, put portions on three plates, and passed them before he sat down.

Holden took his first bite and murmured, "Holly, I will never taste a better." Her eyes danced with some secret amusement, and he wondered what it could be.

Their interrupted talk was still on Imler's mind, for he said, "You better have ample reason to fire Sadler. He's a force in that loosely organized Miners' Union. You'll get plenty of objections from your other work force."

Holden smiled. That put him in control of the talk. "I anticipated that. I fired all of them."

Imler carefully laid down his knife and fork, and the manner with which he did it showed that Holden's announcement startled him.

"That could mean big trouble."

Holden shook his head. "I may have to close down the mill for a few days. No more."

33

Imler's eyes bored like gimlets. "Where will you get more workers? Sadler will blackball—"

Holden grinned. "Not the people I'm planning to hire. They wouldn't even understand him."

Holly's face was puzzled, but Imler knew what he meant. "Ah," he said again. "You're thinking of hiring the Chinese."

Holden laid down his knife. If Imler was thinking of lecturing him again, he was wrong. "You hire them." His tone made it a challenge.

"Yes," Imler admitted. "Drivers, a few shovel men. But not in the skilled jobs."

Holden's face darkened. If he had to put it into plain words, he would. Imler was not going to tell him how to run his mill.

"I'll see that they get what training they need," he said shortly. "Even monkeys pick up tricks."

Holly's eyes flashed at him. "You sound as though you don't think much of them."

Holden shrugged. "Little, grinning men, bowing and scraping. I can handle them."

Somehow that further angered her, for he could see the flush of angry color in her face. She must have something sharp to say, for she showed effort in biting it back.

"If you're shut down too long, you can lose customers," Imler warned.

Holden spaced his words to keep his anger from showing. "I can handle my own affairs."

This was a clash of wills, and it showed in both faces of the men.

"All I can say is you're gambling." Imler's hand on the table was clenched. "Your mill has prospered because of its unique position. You found enough water to run it, and the transportation to others was too far to make the mine owners go anywhere else. But that can change. Practically overnight. The railroad is building here, and that means freighting costs will dwindle. Even if it didn't, somebody might

34

build another mill near here. Particularly if Norborne brings his water into Candelaria."

Holden's face was flushed with open anger. He hadn't given Imler enough credit. The man was aware that water could mean another mill.

"Norborne won't build it," he said savagely. He clamped his lips together. He hadn't intended to let so much vehemence show.

Imler's anger showed in his hooded eyes. "What makes you so positive. I thought the same way when I first heard about his pipeline. Now I'm not so sure. He's already halfway here."

Holden thought that was disapproval in Holly's face, and he was sure he knew its basis. She didn't want him arguing with her father.

He let the charm come back to his face and shrugged. "One of my faults, Holly. I let my tongue run away with me."

"You don't think much of the Chinese?"

He frowned. Surely, she wasn't seeking an argument on that score. She knew the Chinese were inferior people.

His expression was pained. "You're not criticizing me for saying—"

"I am," she said flatly. "I want you to meet one of the grinning monkey people you mentioned." She raised her voice. "Ts'ai, will you please come in here." Her smile actually looked malicious. "We hired a new cook and maid a couple of day ago. I want you to meet Ts'ai Yun."

Holden faced the kitchen door, and his mouth slowly sagged at the sight of the woman momentarily framed in it. She was a tiny thing, not over five feet high, and she couldn't have weighed a hundred pounds. She had the doll-like fragility of some of the Chinese women, and Holden could swear he had never looked at a more beautiful woman. Her olive complexion was flawless, and on her those slant eyes had an unique appeal. Those jet black eyes were expressive with some emotion that could be called fright. In fact, she seemed to cower under it.

Holden's heart suddenly picked up a new, hard thudding.

35

He would not call this woman inferior. He knew that many American males bought Chinese women, but that was in the bordello's. He had looked over those women with disinterest. All of them had been crude, and none of them could compare with this one. He wondered how many American dollars would buy her, and he almost licked his lips, catching himself just in time. He made a vow to himself. In some way, he would know this woman.

Had she heard and understood his remarks about her people? If she had, that would make it harder for him. He dismissed the small concern. Very few of them spoke or understood English.

Holly watched him with a sharper scrutiny. Had some emotion on his face given her a new awareness?

"Ts'ai," Holly said. "This is Mister Holden. You will see him often here."

Ts'ai bobbed her head, but the fright did not leave her eyes. "I am pleased to know you," she said haltingly.

Holden could not keep his greedy eyes off of her. You'll be able to say that with truth, he promised her.

"Mr. Holden made some complimentary remarks about your cooking," Holly said. "I knew you would be pleased to hear that."

"Yes, yes," Ts'ai said rapidly. "I am pleased much to hear it."

She turned suddenly and hurried back into the kitchen.

Holden forced his eyes away from that door. "She is interesting," he said. "It is amazing that she had such ability."

Two pair of eyes watched him, and for a moment, he had the chilling impression that they could read the thoughts in his head.

"Are we going to let this good roast get cold?" He was sure his tone was in the right, light vein. "It only proves what I told you, Dent. These people can be trained."

He made a humorous remark to Holly, and she laughed. Imler only grunted. He could stamp out any little worry that might remain. Things were back to normal.

CHAPTER SIX

Matt and Duncan rode behind the wagons that brought the
Chinese, living and dead, to Candelaria. It was a sorry funeral
procession, he thought morosely, and he wasn't sure what
his part in it was. He hadn't objected to Lo Yen saying that
all the Chinese wanted to leave the camp. The temporary
closedown shut off the drain on his pocket. He wasn't sure
of what Lo Yen wanted to do with the bodies.

The dust in Main Street was fetlock deep, and even this
slow procession stirred it up to hang lazily in the air before
it fell slowly back.

People on the street gave the wagons a casual glance and
no more. Grief that didn't strike them personally didn't rate
a second look.

Candelaria was growing; the traffic on its streets showed it.
Ten saloons did a thriving business, trying to keep up with
the town's thirst. A man could buy a bath in the barbershops,
if he had the money. With water at a dollar a gallon, a
five-dollar bill bought him a skimpy one. Two hotels took
care of the transits, and a half-dozen stores, three lawyers
and as many doctors took care of other various needs. The
two needed three things to retain its growth; the arrival of
the railroad, the piping of water into it, and for the rich
silver veins to hold out. Matt was doing all he could about
the water, and the railroad was driving the spur to Candelaria.
Neither would mean much if the silver veins petered out.
Their failing could turn Candelaria into a ghost town almost
overnight. So far, there wasn't the slightest indication of that.
Even a suggestion of such a thing could set men to jeering.

"What do we do now, Matt?" Duncan asked.

Matt didn't know. "Buy a drink, I guess." He needed a bath, but he wouldn't pay for one at these exorbitant prices.

More Chinese were appearing on the street, and as far as Matt knew an instinct had to draw them. If Lo Yen had sent somebody ahead, Matt hadn't seen or heard about it. But these Chinese knew something was wrong. It was written in the anguished lines of the faces of some of the women. They knew; when it came to a tragedy or a disaster, women had some sixth sense that told them.

He kicked his horse into a faster pace and caught up with the wagon Lo Yen was driving.

The Chinese could be the most inscrutable of people when they wanted to be. Lo Yen looked at him as though he had never seen him before.

"I'll be in town for a while, Lo Yen. Get in touch with me, if there's anything I can do for you."

Lo Yen nodded a grave acceptance of the words; he wanted no more.

It was as Matt suspected. The Chinese took care of their own dead. They neither sought nor wanted outside assistance.

Matt let the wagon pull on ahead. He didn't know when the job would start again. He had another shipment of pipe that would reach Belleville the following week. He would have to be sure of its arrival before he called Lo Yen and the others back. From now on, he was in a grinding race; time required to finish the pipeline against his dollars. He could pay for no more idle time.

He offered to buy Duncan a drink, and Duncan shook his head. "Got some business to attend to, Matt." A sly grin accompanied that, and it told Matt that Duncan's business was personal.

"I'll see you later then, Riley," he said and headed for the saloon across the street. The Roaring Gimlet was his choice because it was the closest.

He stepped into the shadowy interior, and for a brief moment it held the illusion of coolness. But that wouldn't

38

hold. Before a man could finish his first drink sweat would be popping out of him.

The saloon was crowded for this hour of the morning. Matt knew most of them, and he nodded or spoke as he made his way to the end of the bar. If his eyes had been well adjusted to the shadowiness, he wouldn't have stopped here, for it put him next to Ryan Sikeston. Sikeston had every reason not to like him. If Matt's pipeline was successful, it put Sikeston out of business.

Sikeston knew Matt was beside him, but he didn't show it by a word or glance. He had a massive, cadaverous head set on shoulders too small for it. His dull, small eyes were set deeply into the sockets, and his clothes looked as though they were rarely changed. He ran a small freighting business, and in its best times he never used more than two wagons. But he had a profitable thing. He hauled water into town, and there were always more customers than he could supply. If he ran two wagons, he hired three men to help him bucket the water into barrels in the bed of the wagons. Those three men didn't like Matt any better than Sikeston did. If the pipeline was a success, Sikeston was out of business.

Lockwood, on the other side of Sikeston, raised his voice and asked, "Matt, how's the pipeline coming along?" He owned the hardware store, and he had the soft look of an indoor man. His face was round and chubby, and it looked guileless. But Matt knew the man better than to accept outward appearances. The man was a born troublemaker, with a tongue as gossipy as a woman's. There was always a small malice in Lockwood, and it showed now.

Matt heard Sikeston's harsh suck of breath. "All right," he said curtly. He could appreciate how Sikeston felt about him; he had no want to rub it in on him.

The gleam in Lockwood's eyes showed that he had hit sparks. "When do you think it will be?" he persisted. "Or don't you know?"

Sikeston slammed his fist against the bartop, and glasses near him danced. "I can tell you when it'll get here," he shouted. "Never." He was half drunk, and it showed in his eyes and speech.

Matt's cheeks tightened, but he kept his temper. "Maybe you're right, Sikeston. But I'll tell you one thing for sure. You won't have anything to do with stopping it."

He finished his drink and started to step by Sikeston. Sikeston was drunker than he thought. It showed in a loss of usual caution. He grabbed at Matt's arm, and Matt felt the skinny fingers bite into it. "Just what do you mean by that?" he growled.

"If you can't understand English, Sikeston, I haven't got time to teach you. Let go of my arm."

It angered Sikeston beyond bounds, and his fingers only tightened. "Not until you tell me what you mean."

"I mean you're a damned fool," Matt snapped. He knocked Sikeston's hand from his arm and shoved him hard into the bar's edge.

He turned and strode out of the saloon. He started to cross the street to his horse, and he heard the heavy drumming of many hoofs. He whipped his head about, and a sixteen-animal team was pounding down the street, not much more than a half block away. They pulled two, huge ore wagons in tandem behind them, and a Chinese driver sat high on the seat of the first wagon. His mouth was open and strained in some desperate effort, and if he yelled something, Matt couldn't hear it above the savage slam of the hoofs.

It was a runaway, and Matt didn't know what had caused it, but from the look on the driver's face told him that no ordinary method would stop them. Usually the brakes could be depended upon to lock the wheels, putting the great weight of the wagons against the team, but these brakes didn't seem to be working. At a guess he would say that a brake rod had snapped, making the brakes useless.

The driver should have dived from the seat right after the brake rod broke, but apparently, he didn't seem to have that much sense. He was frozen to the seat, sawing on the

40

ineffective reins. This team would run until their shaking legs could not carry them another step, or be stopped by smashing into something that was too solid to give. Matt would say it was the latter. Runaway horses ran in blind panic, and up ahead the street made an abrupt turn, leaving a stone house in the horses' blind course. That driver had better get his horses around the turn, and Matt didn't know how he was going to do it.

People, up ahead, darted out of the street and dived for the nearest doorway. A couple of dogs yipped frantically as they scuttled out of the street. That was all anybody could do right now, and Matt half-turned back toward the saloon's door. His eyes widened in horror. The baby had appeared out of nowhere and was now toddling deeper into the street. Its unsteady steps marked it as being about two years old, and Matt couldn't tell whether it was boy or girl. All he could be sure was that it was Chinese. No white kid was dressed like this.

He yelled a hoarse, strangled warning, realizing that even if the baby heard him it would mean nothing to it.

The hard pound of hoofs was drowning out everything else, and Matt did not dare check the closeness of the team, knowing that it would melt his first impulse.

He was in a full run with his first step toward the baby. He had no definite plan of action; the time was too short to even try to think of one. He only knew that his margin was terribly thin. The pound of hoofs seemed much louder, threatening to burst his eardrums. At any split second he expected to feel the bone-breaking impact as the first two horses smashed into him.

He had a last, fleeting impression of sloe eyes staring up at him, the mouth opened wide in the first of the frightened howls. He bent low, scooped up the child in his arms, and he thought he was going to get completely clear. One leg was extended behind him, and something clipped that heel to send him spinning. He flew through the air, trying to hunch his shoulders lower and wrap his arms tighter to pro-

41

tect the baby. He lit on one shoulder and rolled, and the impact clicked his teeth together and rattled his brains.

That wall of blackness wanted him; it kept reaching for him, and he fought it off. He vaguely heard the kid's yowling, and he didn't know whether hurt or just terror was back of it.

He came to a stop on his back still holding the youngster. It cried in animal-like yowls, its eyes squinted shut, its mouth opened wide. Could a baby cry that lustily, if it was hurt?

He heard a crash from the end of the street and didn't have to turn his head to know what it was. The horses had run into the stone house.

He gently shook the baby. "Hey, old-timer, it's all over. You can stop that now."

He sat up, shaking his head until the blackness sullenly retreated. He had saved the kid, but what was he going to do with it now?"

A Chinese woman darted out of the nearest doorway and rushed to him. A terror twisted her face too, and Matt couldn't make a sane word out of the torrent of sound that poured from her mouth.

He tried to grin at her. "I don't think he's hurt."

She tore the baby out of his arms, whirled, and ran back toward the door. The torrent of sound had never ceased, and Matt grinned ruefully as he watched her disappear. He hadn't recognized a word she said.

He stood and swore softly at the stab of pain that shot up his right leg from the ankle. He took another step and sucked in his breath. The ankle was tender. One of those horses had solidly clipped him. He took another step and kept the wince off of his face. It would serve him, if he didn't get too reckless with it.

People poured out all along the street and ran toward the crashup. Matt limped after them.

Twenty people were around the wreck by the time he reached it. He had never seen a worse one. Dead and dying horses were piled up against the stone wall, and threshing hoofs slashed the air. The two ore wagons' momentum had plowed through the horses until the wall stopped them, too. One might be repaired; the other was a total loss. The driver had been tossed onto the pile of mangled flesh, and Matt couldn't tell how badly he had been hurt. Then a slashing hoof caught the man in the body and answered Matt's question, for he heard neither sound nor saw further movement.

One of the bystanders said, "Well, that's another of the furrin bastards gone."

Matt didn't know the man, and he stared somberly at him.

The man colored under the accusation in Matt's eyes and said angrily, "Goddamn it! Ain't we got enough of them around?"

Some of the onlookers believed as the man did, for Matt heard verbal echo to the man's words. Matt wouldn't say that compassion was an overwhelming trait of the human being.

He turned and limped back down the street. He could stand another drink. He thought of the Chinese he had brought into town just a little while ago. Now another one could be added. That made four dead, and it should please the big-mouth who had commented on the dead driver. Matt shook his head and tried to forget about it. He imagined quite a few Chinese women would be grieving tonight.

CHAPTER SEVEN

Matt didn't realize how battered he was until he leaned against the welcome support of the bar. Each muscle seemed to have received its special malevolent attention.

"Whiskey, Sam," he ordered from the bartender. The whiskey wouldn't ease the aching muscles, but it might dull their protests.

More men filed into the saloon, and they were filled with chatter about the wreck. Matt moved farther along the bar, not wanting to become involved in their talk. He already had enough of it at the scene.

"That'll cost Imler a pretty penny," one of them said.

"Hell, he can afford it," another replied.

None of them said anything about the dead driver, and no one mentioned the kid involved. Apparently, they hadn't seen Matt's rescue. It suited him just as well.

He downed the second glass, feeling its relaxing warmth stealing through him. He hadn't noticed until now that he was a mess. The tear he had received in the right leg of his pants during yesterday's climb had been lengthened, and the left knee was torn out. One sleeve was almost ripped off, and his face felt stiff and stinging. He touched the caked dirt on it, and blood still oozed from his cheek. No wonder that Sam had looked oddly at him.

Dirt was ground into both arms, and he cursed at this new drain on his money. He couldn't go around looking like this. He needed a bath and new clothes. Damnit! He had hoped to get several more months' wear out of these garments.

He finished his third drink, nodded his thanks to Sam, and walked out. He stopped in at Ralston's Emporium, and

Tate Ralston asked, "What happened to you? You look like you've been in a wreck."

Matt grinned ruefully. "Tate, I need a new pair of pants and a shirt."

Ralston nodded. "I can fix you up."

Matt bought a new pair of jeans and a blue shirt. Nothing fancy about them, but he would look respectable.

He paid Ralston and carried the new shirt and pants out with him. Clem Novinger was his regular barber, and he walked toward his shop.

Novinger wasn't doing anything when Matt walked in, and Matt shook his head at the offer of the chair.

"A bath first, Clem. Then I'll see how I look."

Novinger was an aging man but still spry with humor in his face. "You look like you could use it. Hot or cold?"

Matt sighed. The hot cost twenty-five cents more, but the cold wouldn't be able to touch the dirt ground into him.

"Hot," he answered. He would have to wait for that. It would take some time to heat the water.

"John," Novinger called, and a grinning Chinese boy stuck his head through the rear door of the shop. Novinger looked at Matt. "How many?"

"Five gallons," Matt replied. It wouldn't be enough to soak in, but it would have to do.

"Velly quick," John promised and withdrew.

"A good boy," Novinger said. The speculation in his eyes grew. "You look like you've been in a wreck."

"You could call it that," Matt said wryly. Novinger would never forgive him for not telling him about the crashup, but get him started on something, and he never stopped. He sat down, ignoring the papers on the chair next to him. At best, those papers would be weeks old, and he had probably read most of them.

Novinger was a garrulous man, and he never lost an opportunity to talk. "Did you hear about Steiger?"

Matt shook his head. He wasn't interested in anything

45

Steiger did. Someday, someone would have to put a bullet in Steiger's head.

"They found him yesterday afternoon," Novinger said with relish. "Had a bullet in his head."

That almost pulled a grin out of Matt. He hadn't heard of Novinger having the ability to read thoughts.

"Who did it?"

Novinger shrugged. "Nobody knows."

Matt grunted. Steiger's reputation was well known. He had earned that bullet. "Small loss."

Novinger rattled on about the things he knew and the rumors he had heard about Steiger. "Bound to happen," he said cheerfully. "The town's better off. You know I hated to see him come in here. You wouldn't believe what I've found in his hair."

Matt probably would, but he didn't want to hear about it. "No loss," he repeated.

Novinger vigorously bobbed his head. "I agree with that. I didn't need or wanted his business."

And didn't dare to say so, Matt thought. Steiger had lived a violent life. His end wasn't surprising.

John stuck his head back through the door. "Leady."

The water wouldn't be hot, not in this short time. But it was probably the best Matt could hope for. He walked into the rear room, and John was just pouring the last bucket into the wooden, zinc-lined tub. It was a big, clumsy thing, and a man had ample room to stretch out in it. Matt put a sour eye on the water level. He should have doubled that order. He chased that thought out of his head. He was already spending enough money because of that wreck.

He stripped off his clothes and eased into the water. His caution wasn't necessary. The water was only pleasantly warm.

He reached for the big yellow bar of soap, and John said, "I sclub back."

Matt shook his head. "Not until I wash my face." He didn't want the water to change too much color before he did that.

The soapy water increased the stinging in his cheek. He touched it and felt its rawness. He had probably just scraped some skin, but it could hurt as much as a more serious wound.

"You hurt?" John asked solicitously. He made an L out of the R again.

"No," Matt said shortly. He didn't want to talk about it. He handed the soap to John. That would cost him a tip.

At least, his back didn't hurt. He sat there, watching the water slowly darken. He had picked up a lot of Candelaria's dust.

He took the bar from the Chinese and soaped himself thoroughly. Five gallons of water would be adequate and no more.

He finished his bath and stood. What he really needed now was another five gallons of fresh water. A man could be a dirty animal.

John looked at the bath water and cackled. "Plenty dilty."

Matt couldn't fuss with that. The water was a thin mud. He dried himself with a rough husk towel and tossed it to John. His skin had a pleasant tingling. A man needed to do this about once a day.

He dressed in the new clothes, transfered the contents of the pockets of the old pants, and put a quarter into John's hand. John seemed pleased, for he stood there, bobbing his head, a wide grin on his face. Matt wondered what kind of a living the boy had. Hell, he thought impatiently. He had enough to worry about his own.

"Throw them away." He indicated the old clothes. John might disobey that, finding some small service left in them. Either way, it didn't matter to Matt.

He walked into the outer room, and Novinger said hopefully, "A shave, Matt?"

Matt shook his head. Not with this scraped cheek. He would be looking pretty rough before that cheek could stand the touch of a razor.

Nothing dampened Novinger's spirits. "Next time then, Matt."

47

Matt nodded and walked outside. He stood there, not certain of what he should do next. It would be some time before he could expect to see Riley Duncan again. Duncan was a lucky man to be able to get rid of his stresses so easily.

He started to move on, and Lo Yen came around the corner. Matt was surprised to see him so soon. He didn't know how long a Chinese funeral took, but surely, it couldn't be over this soon.

"You looking for me, Lo Yen?" He didn't need to ask that. The expression on Lo Yen's face told him that.

"All over town," Lo Yen said, and that was urgency in his tone. "Come with me, please." Lo Yen spoke good English, the R's seemed to cause him the trouble most Chinese had.

Matt fell into step with him. He would find out soon enough why Lo Yen wanted him.

Lo Yen led him to the cluster of shacks at the south end of town. They were poor, miserable hovels, and Matt knew it was the best the Chinese could afford.

Lo Yen stopped at the doorway of one of them and waited for Matt to enter ahead of him. It was a bare little room, but the earthen floor had been scrupulously swept. Another room had been partitioned off with a muslin curtain, and from behind it Matt heard a woman's crying.

"My sister," Lo Yen said quietly at the look Matt gave him.

The few items of furniture didn't erase the impression of the room's bareness. In the middle of it a figure was stretched out on a blanket. Matt didn't have to approach it to know the man was dead. The quietness of it screamed it at him.

The man had been stripped to the waist, and his back was covered with dark, ugly bruises.

Matt couldn't see the face, but he knew who it was. "Kung," he said sharply. Was this the way the Chinese laid out their dead?

Lo Yen nodded. "His wife found something when she cleaned him up. I thought you should see it."

Matt didn't want to approach the body. He had seen it before, and he knew how cruelly Kung had been battered.

Lo Yen pointed out the purplish hole between Kung's shoulder's blades.

Matt sucked in his breath and said an unnecessary thing. "He's been shot."

That seemed to relieve some anxiety in Lo Yen's face. "I thought so, too. His wife will be glad to know that he wasn't responsible for the loss of your wagon."

"He isn't," Matt grimly agreed. He could see it almost as plainly as though he had been there at the moment the wagon had gone over. Kung had reared up under the impact of the bullet, and his hold on the reins had jerked the teams over the edge. He squatted to more closely examine the bullet wound.

He looked up at Lo Yen and asked, "Do you know—"

It wasn't necessary to finish the question, nor did Lo Yen have to answer it. Lo Yen didn't know.

Matt straightened, and his face was a hard mask. "I'll find out who did it, Lo Yen." Maybe he was premature in making that statement, but a name flashed into his mind. Sikeston! It fitted the threats Sikeston had made in the bar.

He gripped Lo Yen's shoulder for a brief moment. This was Lo Yen's brother-in-law, and Matt hadn't even known that a relation had existed between them.

That was a bitter determination in Lo Yen's eyes, and Matt wouldn't name Sikeston until he knew.

"Is there anything else I can do, Lo Yen?"

Lo Yen shook his head. "But I would like to know."

"Sure," Matt said gently. But it wasn't all Lo Yen's business now. It was his.

"Are you sure I can't do anything for you?"

"Nothing," Lo Yen replied. But there was some kind of an appeal in his eyes.

Matt stopped briefly at the doorway. The woman's crying carried clearly to it.

49

CHAPTER EIGHT

Though he wasn't looking for him, Matt ran across Riley Duncan an hour later in the Roaring Gimlet Saloon. This was the third time he had been in here since he had talked to Lo Yen, and he knew a familiar disappointment. Sikeston wasn't here.

Duncan talked animatedly to the man on his left, and he had the indolent, happy expression of a satisfied man. It was too bad, but Matt was going to shatter that mood.

He touched Duncan, and Duncan said with feeling, "Matt. I was hoping to run into you. I'll buy a beer."

"Not now," Matt said. "I've got to talk to you."

One sweeping look decided Duncan that Matt was serious, but he offered a minor argument. "Just as soon as I finish my beer."

"Now," Matt said impatiently.

"Must be a hell of a rush," Duncan grumbled as he walked outside with Matt. "Hey!" His eyes widened. "You've bought some new clothes."

Matt waved that aside. It would take too long to explain, and he had far more important things on his mind.

"Kung was shot," he said abruptly. "In the back. By the size of the hole I'd say a rifle did it."

Duncan's jaw sagged. "Aw hell, Matt. It couldn't be."

"I saw it," Matt snapped. He told of going with Lo Yen to see the body. "His wife found it when she cleaned him up. I guess she didn't want him buried the way he looked."

Duncan looked as though this was beyond his grasp. "Maybe it was an accident."

Matt snorted. "A rifle shot in the back?"

"I guess not," Duncan muttered. "But who would want—"

"That's what I'm going to find out."

"You think Kung had enemies?"

The impatience came back to Matt's fac[e] incidental. He was just caught up in some[

His exasperation spread as he saw Duncan "Can't you see it? Somebody wanted our w[the edge. Can you think of a better way than to shoot the driver on that turn?"

Duncan floundered through Matt's words. "But who do you think would want that?"

"Sikeston for one. Probably the biggest one. He made some threats about what he was going to do to stop me." His eyes had that cold, brilliant shine. "Maybe he's already started."

Duncan's swearing was a low rumbling of sound. "Why, goddamn him. I'll break his neck."

"We've got to find him first. I've been looking for him. Maybe he took his wagon out for another load of water."

"Then we'll wait for him until he gets back," Duncan said savagely.

"We can spend the time to better advantage." Matt had no hope of finding somebody who had seen Sikeston fire that shot. But if he could establish that Sikeston was out of town yesterday, it would be a big, forward step.

"Ask around town," he instructed Duncan. "See if you can find out where he was yesterday afternoon. I'll meet you here in an hour or so."

"I'll find out," Duncan said grimly as he started out.

Matt watched him stalk away. He hoped Duncan didn't run across Sikeston after he found out that he was out of town yesterday. That would be enough for Duncan to try to make good his threat against Sikeston.

He went in the opposite direction, stopping in every saloon to ask if Sikeston was in yesterday. At each negative answer his elation grew. Maybe it wasn't conclusive proof, but it was support.

Jude Cummings, in the Red Garter, dashed it. "Sure, he was in here. Spent all yesterday afternoon. The way he was

..ng, I thought I'd have to carry him out. He stood right .ere you are, wailing about the money he was losing. His wagon was being repaired."

Disappointment flooded Matt's face. "Are you sure, Jude?"

"Damnit! I served and listened to him all afternoon, didn't I? If you don't believe me, ask Horton. He repaired Sikeston's wagon."

"I'll do that," Matt said, but all of the elation was gone. Jude's words weren't something a man would just make up out of thin air.

Neal Horton laid down his hammer as Matt walked into his blacksmith shop. He was a brawny man, the long years of work at his trade showing in his shoulders and arms. He mopped his face and said, "As hot as it is in this country, I've got to pick this kind of work."

Matt didn't respond to the wry humor. "Neal, was Sikeston in here yesterday afternoon?"

Horton squinted at him. "A half-dozen times. He lets his equipment go until it's ready to fall apart. Then he expects me to turn it out in a couple of minutes. I put new rims on two wheels and replaced several spokes. It's a good thing I did. His team would have been pulling his wagon along on its axles." He closed one eye calculatingly. "How come you're so interested? I wouldn't say it was because of any fondness between you."

"No," Matt said in dull agreement. He could cross off Sikeston's name from his list. Sikeston was a wagon man. Matt could never remember seeing him riding a horse. The sad part of it was that when he crossed off Sikeston's name, there went the entire list.

"Thanks, Jude."

Horton shrugged and picked up his hammer. "Anytime, Matt."

Matt walked outside, and Duncan was coming toward him. There was no lift in Duncan's face. Evidently, what he had learned wasn't what he wanted.

"I asked in the restaurants, Matt. He ate breakfast and sup-

52

per in Candelaria. He couldn't have covered that ride in one day."

"He didn't," Matt said wearily. He told Duncan what he had heard from Horton. "Sikeston never left town yesterday," he finished.

Duncan had a tenacious grip on an idea when he got hold of it. "That doesn't mean he couldn't have hired somebody else."

"It doesn't," Matt agreed. He recalled what Novinger had told him about Steiger. Steiger was rumored to be a likely man for the kind of job that had killed Kung. But then Steiger was dead, and if there was a link between him and Sikeston, Matt wouldn't find it. Had Steiger been killed to stop his mouth? Matt briefly toyed with the question, then let it slip away. For a moment, he was tempted to beat it out of Sikeston, but he would be sticking his neck out too far, if nothing came from it. At the least, Sikeston would have him thrown into jail, and it would probably cost Matt a fine.

"What will we do now, Matt?" The helplessness in Duncan's voice said he needed guidance.

Matt gave him a pained grin. "I'd say eat supper."

"You're not going to forget about it," Duncan protested.

No, Matt wouldn't forget about it. Every dollar he paid out would remind him of it. Already, his margin was too thin.

CHAPTER NINE

Matt didn't know which awakened him; the throbbing headache, or the noise blasting at his ears. He fought coming back to awareness. He only wished he could return to that blessed unconscious. He groaned as thoughts filtered slowly into his head. A man was so vulnerable to the morning afterward.

He grabbed his head, trying to ease its throbbing. It seemed to start at his teeth, then climbed for the top of his head, gathering force as it moved. That noise continued, and he winced each time he heard it. It sounded like a saw blade hitting an oak knot, screeching futilely for a moment, then shattering into a thousand pieces with a deafening noise. Then after the briefest of silences, it started all over again.

He ran his tongue around his mouth and grimaced. He knew what that swamper in the saloon last night had done with his sweepings. He had put them in his mouth. Why was a man such a damned fool when it came to liquor? He never knew when he had exactly enough; he had to take that one more drink that cut all of the solid ground from beneath his feet. He knew how it had started, though he wasn't using it as an excuse. But he had been tired and depressed, and he had taken a couple of drinks after supper to ease both conditions. The first few drinks had lifted him, and if a few drinks did that much, why not more?

He put a jaundiced eye on Duncan, lying beside him. "You sure as hell weren't any help," he said sourly. "You kept saying, just one more."

He could have yelled that, and Duncan wouldn't have heard him. His mouth was open with his snoring, and each

54

time the saw blade hit that knot, Matt shuddered. Duncan was an easy man when it came to drowning his worries.

Matt swore at his unsteadiness as he got out of bed. Even if he could have awakened Duncan, he didn't want to. He had had enough of Duncan's company for a while. He grinned ruefully as he thought, Duncan could have probably said the same thing about him with emphasis.

He looked at his woeful reflection in the mirror. "If you aren't a God-awful mess," he said to it. "And you didn't solve a damned thing."

He really needed a shave this morning, but the scraped cheek was beginning to scab over. He winced at the thought of a razor pulling at it.

He emptied the water pitcher into the bowl and dunked his head in it. He came up sputtering and blowing, but his head was clearer. He scowled about the hotel room. For a man who was concerned about his finances he hadn't shown much of it last night.

He dressed with care, and his head stayed on his shoulders. He would come back after Duncan in an hour or two. They were not going to pay for another day in this room.

He walked into the lobby, and Hardy, the day clerk, was on duty.

"What time is it, Hardy?" he asked in a hollow voice.

Hardy grinned. He had seen a lot of men in this condition, and he found a macabre humor at the way Matt must feel.

"Ten o'clock, Matt. I thought you two were going to sleep the day through."

Matt glared at him. Why was a man's suffering so funny to others? "Did we cause any trouble when we came in last night?"

"Priam said you did." Priam was the night clerk. "He said he and you had a hell of a time getting Duncan up the stairs. He couldn't get Duncan to stop his singing. He was sure it would awaken the whole town."

Maybe it would be funny tomorrow; it wasn't now. "I'll come back for him shortly," Matt said.

"If you're thinking of breakfast, you missed it."

Matt groaned hollowly at the thought of food. "I just want coffee. It's not too late for that, is it?"

Hardy took the grin off of his face, but it lurked behind his eyes. "I guess you can get that," he conceded.

Matt walked outdoors, and the sun was a club against his tender head. He was glad he didn't see anybody he knew. He didn't want any talk, either.

He headed for Mrs. Grunson's Restaurant across the street. Her food wasn't good, and her coffee was in the same class, but Matt doubted if his taste buds were working this morning.

Mrs. Grunson was the only one in the room when Matt entered. She was a buxom woman, and her face was on the shrew side. But then, she probably had her troubles like everybody else.

"Breakfast's over," she said with asperity. She acted as though his entrance was an affront. Maybe that was a big part of her poor business.

"Just coffee, Mrs. Grunson."

She sniffed and waddled to the stove. Her weight was making an increasing demand on her legs. She brought back the blackened pot and poured him a cup.

He sipped at it and managed to keep his face blank. It was last night's coffee, warmed over and as strong as hell to a sinner. He was wrong about his taste buds not working.

She wasn't in the mood for talk, and that suited him just fine. He had some things to sort out in his head.

The next shipment of pipe wouldn't arrive at Belleville for another five days. He had thought he had been so clever in spacing them out, but it had kicked him in the face. The thought of all that empty time didn't help the queasiness in his stomach.

He ordered another cup. The strong black coffee was what he needed. He was beginning to feel like a human being again.

"Good coffee, Mrs. Grunson," he said as he paid for it.

That almost smoothed out her face, but it didn't quite make it.

He walked outside, and he could stand the sun a little better. He was a man who liked work, and the void ahead of him left him frustrated. Maybe he should drag in the wagons and have Horton give them a goingover.

He had about decided that was the right course when Solly Tipton hailed him from across the street, then hurried over. Matt's knowledge of the man was confined to an occasional drink with him. Tipton worked for Dent Imler, but Matt didn't know exactly what he did. Maybe that was the path a man should pick, go to work for a rich man. He wouldn't have to worry constantly about the source of his money—if he could hold onto the job. He didn't know what Tipton wanted, but if he suggested a drink, Matt would clobber him.

"Solly," he said and nodded.

Tipton returned the greeting. He was a tall, lean man with a suggestion of softness about him. Even if his hands said he was unfamiliar with manual labor, his clothes did. A man didn't wear these kind of clothes on a rough job. Maybe he worked in Imler's office. Imler would need somebody to keep up with his paper work.

"I've been looking all over town for you," Tipton said. He had an aggrieved note in his voice as though Matt was deliberately responsible for the long search. "Dent wants to see you." He added as an afterthought, "You know he isn't a man who likes to be kept waiting."

Matt frowned. So what? He was tempted to tell Tipton what he could do with it, then reconsidered. He knew Dent Imler only to nod to, but then, it wasn't wise to offend a man of Imler's standing. Besides, his curiosity prodded him. Maybe Imler wanted to know the details of the wreck of his ore wagons. Matt wasn't the man to tell him. He had been too involved in saving a slant-eyed kid.

"What's he want?" he asked crossly.

Tipton laughed. "I don't ask Dent questions. I just take his orders. He's waiting for you at his house. Do you know where

57

it it? He told me to find you before I went to work." Some anxiety worked on him as he asked, "You'll see him right away?"

Matt could cause him a little mental hell by saying, I'll think about it. He discarded it. Tipton was an innocent bystander. He shouldn't be caught in the crossfire of Matt's bad feelings and Dent's imperiousness.

"I'll see him. Do I have to run all the way?"

Tipton flushed at the sardonic words. "Hell, Matt. I'm only trying to do what I'm paid for."

"Sure," Matt said gently. Maybe Tipton's course wasn't the best way. An employer's idiosyncrasies could chaff a man.

Tipton looked back anxiously after a dozen strides. Matt gave him a reassuring wave. Damnit! He was going.

An unavoidable awe filled him at the sight of Imler's house. It was something to see. He had not been in it before. He began criticizing his clothes. He should have brought something better, and then he swore at himself. He didn't have to make apologies for his appearance.

He knocked on the door with unneeded force. He knew Imler had a daughter. He had seen her a couple of times in town, though he had never spoken to her.

It seemed he waited too long, and he raised his knuckles again. How long did Imler think he could keep him standing out here?

The door opened while his hand was upraised, and he felt foolish and awkward.

This was Holly Imler, and she was an attractive woman. A glint of amusement danced in her eyes, and he thought he knew what she was thinking.

Her words confirmed it. "Really, Mr. Norborne. I answered the door as fast as I could."

She must think him an impatient clown, and he was surprised that she knew him. His face colored, and he mumbled, "I thought you didn't hear me. Tipton said your father wanted to see me."

58

"He does," she said gravely, but the glint remained in her eyes. She stepped aside for him to enter.

He removed his hat with a clumsy hand, and he felt ill-at-ease. She was laughing at him, and it stirred his anger.

"This way," she said and led the way to the parlor.

If he thought the outside of the house was something, he should have waited until he got inside. Everything in it screamed money.

Dent Imler got up as Matt entered the room. His craggy face didn't soften, but he thrust out of his hand.

Matt took it. This was no soft hand; Imler had the grip of a man long used to hard work.

"I thought Tipton couldn't find you. I sent him out a couple of hours ago."

Both of them watched him with appraising eyes, and Matt bristled. Was Imler blaming him for not getting here on the run? He couldn't tell them the real reason it had taken Tipton so long, and he said flatly, "I was busy." He groaned mentally at the figure he must be cutting before her.

"It doesn't matter," Imler said. "Were you near that wreck yesterday?"

Was Imler fighting some claim because of the dead driver? If so, he was going to be disappointed. Matt didn't intend to put any blame on the driver.

"Your wagons passed me. It was a runaway. I'd say the brake rod had broken. I didn't actually see the wreck."

Imler gave him a frosty grin as though he guessed at the reasons behind Matt's words.

"I'm not interested in the wreck. Somebody rescued a Chinese baby. I heard it was you."

The abrupt change in the trend of the talk left Matt fumbling. "Why?"

Imler's patience didn't crack. "If it was you, somebody would like to thank you. She's the wife of your driver who was killed."

Matt tried to retain his stiffness. Nothing about this was

59

going the way he thought it would. "Kung's wife?" He had heard her crying yesterday; he hadn't seen her.

Imler nodded. "She works for us. That would have made a terrible day for her. First, her husband, then her son. She leaves him with her aunt while she works here. The aunt told her about it, but he didn't know who you were." He smiled for the first time, a warm, sincere thing. "It took some digging to locate you. I talked to some men who thought you were an idiot to risk your life the way you did."

Matt relaxed. "I was just the closest," he said, disclaiming any special credit.

Holly smiled with open approval of him. "We think it's more than that. Ts'ai wants to thank you."

Matt tried to wave it aside. "It isn't necessary—"

"It is to her," Holly said softly. Her eyes ran over him in frank appraisal, and she didn't see anything she disapproved of.

"Ts'ai," she called.

Ts'ai came into the room. She was beautiful woman, though her face was marked with her grieving. She was a fragile, doll-like creature, and Matt thought, I could hold her in one palm. It was hard to think of her as a wife and mother.

"This is Mr. Norborne, Ts'ai," Holly said. "The one who saved your baby."

Words poured out of Ts'ai, almost too rapid and broken for Matt to understand. She saw by his face that she was going too fast, and she said, "Please! My English is not good."

"It's just fine," he said awkwardly. "I was glad I was around." He hunted for something that would ease her grief, and he blurted out, "Kung was a fine man."

"Yes," she said simply as tears welled into her eyes. "But without my son I could not have stood it. You will find the man who killed my husband?"

He hated to shatter her hopes. "I'm trying," he answered.

He turned his head at the knock on the door. Holly looked exasperated at the interruption. It was a relief to Matt.

"Get rid of whoever it is, Ts'ai," Imler ordered.

She scurried out of the room, and Imler regarded Matt with open favor. He seemed to be searching for the right words, and Holly broke in. "Don't play it down, Mr. Norborne. Can't you think of how crushed she would have been?"

Matt nodded. He need erect no barriers against these two. "How does anybody say they're sorry to somebody like her?"

Holly smiled. "You did just fine."

Imler frowned at him. "I thought her husband was killed in a wreck. What did she mean by what she asked you?"

"He was shot. I didn't know until I visited their house yesterday. I didn't see her then. In a way, I'm responsible. Whoever did it wanted a wagonload of pipe to go over the mountain."

He was looking at Imler, but he heard Holly suck in her breath."

"Ah," Imler murmured. "To stop your building. Will it?"

"It will not," Matt said savagely. He wished he could tell Imler how it had strained him. He just wished he had a small part of Imler's resources.

"Please," Ts'ai said from the doorway. "I told him. But he would not listen."

Matt was sure he saw a hardening in Imler's face before he looked at Gary Holden. The man brushed by Ts'ai as he entered the room.

"I knew she didn't mean me," Holden said.

Matt looked at him with speculative eyes. The man seemed to have a special standing in this house, and somehow Matt felt a sense of loss.

Holly's displeasure showed, too. "Oh Gary," she started, then changed it. "Mr. Norborne is here for Ts'ai to thank him. He saved her baby from one of our runaway wagons."

"Ah," Holden said. "I've heard of Mr. Norborne." He didn't offer to shake hands.

Matt's eyes sharpened. Was there a hidden meaning in Holden's words? He decided not. He was getting highly suspicious of everyone. He had never had any contact with Holden, and from this brief exchange, he didn't want to.

Odd currents were in this room, and he wished he could read the thoughts behind all these eyes. He thought he could safely say that Imler didn't hold Holden in high esteem. He wished he felt as sure about Holly. That sense of loss grew.

"I would say that Ts'ai was a fortunate woman," Holden said. He smiled ingratiatingly at her.

The words had a hollow ring, and Matt felt sorry for Holly. He didn't know what her interest in Holden was, but he would say that it was worthless. Holden stared too long at Ts'ai. She felt it too, for her face was flustered under his eyes. A woman had an instinct or a sixth sense for this.

"Excuse," she said, hurried across the room, and disappeared.

Holden's eyes never left her until she was gone.

Matt had seen men look at a woman before like this. The bastard, he thought, and it gave him a mild shock. He wants her.

Holly couldn't have missed that, and Matt didn't look at her, afraid that he would see the hurt in her eyes.

Holden looked back at Matt and asked easily, "How's your pipeline coming along?"

"Fine." Matt's tone was curt. He probed again for some reason behind the question. It certainly wasn't friendly interest. "I'll finish it."

"Good," Imler said with hearty approval.

Holden flashed him a veiled glance. At the least, that annoyed him.

Matt wondered if he could outsit Holden and was tempted to try it. At best, he would only increase the embarrassment that was rife in the room.

He got to his feet. "I'll keep in touch with Ts'ai. I wish there was more I could do for her." He started for the door.

"I'll go with you," Holly said. Her head was held regally high as though she was fighting off some flooding hurt.

Matt shook his head, and she said, "But I want to."

That put more than annoyance in Holden, and Matt grinned.

Where did this desire to sting this man come from? "That would be just fine," he said.

He stopped at the outer door. "If there's anything I can do—" His words faded.

She squarely met his eyes. "I'll let you know."

He tried to make something more out of the words. Was there some kind of a promise in them? "She's lucky to be working for you," he said, touched his hat, and turned. He looked back at the end of the walk, and she was still in the doorway. He raised his hand, and she returned the wave.

All of a sudden he felt good. The miserable squeamishness was gone from his stomach, and he felt oddly happy. He loked back again, and the door was closed. He grinned at himself. Did he expect her to still be there?

CHAPTER TEN

Duncan was awake when Matt entered the room, and he looked at Matt with a jaundiced eye. "What have you got to look so damned happy about?" he growled.

"I don't know," Matt said honestly. Could a few words with Holly Imler make this change in the day?

"I waited breakfast for you," he said.

Duncan groaned as he swung his legs to the floor. He raised his head from his hands and squinted at Matt. "What happened to you? I've had to baby you before after a night like last one."

"You're still dreaming," Matt jeered at him. "You never saw the day you had to take care of me." Both of them knew that was a lie, but at the moment, he had the upper hand.

"Are you coming?" he demanded. "I'm hungry." He was, suddenly, ravenously hungry. "How does eggs and ham sound to you?" He wouldn't go back to Mrs. Grunson's. She could do enough damage to just a cup of coffee.

A spasm of nausea crossed Duncan's face, and he whimpered, "You're a damned torturer."

Matt grinned innocently. "I don't know what you're talking about."

He waited until Duncan dressed and shaved. "At least, I can do something you can't do," Duncan said. "Your face is a mess."

Matt touched the stiffening of the scab on his cheek. He wondered what Imler and Holly thought about it; neither of them had said a word.

"Why does a man do such damned fool things, Matt?" Duncan asked as they went out of the door.

Matt laughed. "I wouldn't have missed it for the world."

Half of that was true. He wouldn't have missed the last thirty minutes of it.

They went to Burrill's Cafe, and Herb Burrill gave them a big hello. He was a short, plump man with a beaming face. If he ate here, he enjoyed his cooking.

Matt jerked his head toward Duncan. "Herb, have you get anything for an ailing man."

Burrill studied the bad color in Duncan's face, the dark hollows beneath his eyes. He stepped back before he made his diagnosis. If the visible evidence wasn't enough, the reek of Duncan's breath was. "A potful of strong black coffee. And a couple of days without repeating what he did last night."

Duncan snarled at him. "Everybody's trying to be so damned funny."

Matt ordered ham and eggs and upon second thought, added a stack of wheats to it.

Duncan shuddered when Burrill brought the food to the table. "That makes me sick."

Matt grinned in broad amusement. "You're blaming the wrong thing."

He drowned the stack of wheats in syrup and tore into his food. It was amazing how low a man could feel one moment, then so much higher the next.

Duncan looked brighter after he drank three cups of coffee. He eyed the remaining ham on Matt's plate. "That looks good."

Matt pushed his plate toward him. "Help yourself."

Duncan forked the ham and lifted it to his mouth. He sniffed it with an animal's wariness, and Matt's grin grew. "It won't poison you."

Duncan chewed it with caution, swallowed, then said in wonder, "That's good. I didn't think I'd ever eat again, or at least, for a whole week." He turned his head toward Burrill. "Herb, I'll have an order of ham and eggs."

Burrill's diagnosis was wrong. Duncan wouldn't need two days to recover.

65

Matt watched in admiration as Duncan packed in the food. "How about a drink after we're through eating?"

Duncan missed the sarcasm in Matt's question and gave it careful consideration. He shook his head. "Not right now. Give me a couple more hours, then ask me."

"Someday, it's going to kill you."

"I thought it had this morning," Duncan confessed. He took the warning complacently. "If it doesn't, something else will. I'm ready to go."

Matt paid the bill and scowled at the change Burrill put in his hand.

"Something wrong, Matt?" Burrill asked.

"Everything was fine," Matt assured him. But living in town wasn't. It was too damned expensive.

They walked outside, and Duncan belched in contented satisfaction. "It doesn't take much to revive a man, does it?"

"Depends upon what a man's looking for," Matt said. He started to add something to that, and Ta'si came out of the store, across the street, her arms laden with packages.

Matt watched her with idle attention. "That's Kung's widow, Riley. I met her at the Imler house. She works for them." His grin had a trace of embarrassment in it. "She wanted to thank me for saving her son."

"She's a tiny little thing, isn't she?" Duncan said in reverent awe. "Life must be tough on her."

"She'll make out." She was lucky she worked for the Imlers. They would look after her. He would add to it whatever he could, but it would be nothing compared to the Imlers' help.

Ts'ai had stopped at the corner. She looked behind her as though she wanted to flee, and his eyes narrowed. What did she see?

Holden came around the corner, and his face was creased in a smile. He spoke to her, and she didn't want to talk to him. Matt couldn't see her face, but her attitude said that she was frightened.

66

Holden reached out for the packages in her arms, and she jerked them away.

"Wait here for me, Riley," Matt said and crossed the street.

"Let me help you, Ts'ai," he heard Holden say as he approached them.

"Trouble, Ts'ai?" Matt asked. She turned her face to him and gasped. That was relief on her face.

"No, no," she said hurriedly. "I must go now." She scurried past Holden.

Holden's face was stiff with anger. "What the hell do you think you're doing?" he asked with fury. "I was only trying to help her."

"She didn't want your help," Matt said softly. His face reflected more than an echo of Holden's anger. What did this damned fool think he was going to do; carry those packages right up to the Imler house? His anger increased. What would Holly think or do when she saw Holden?

"By God, you'd better learn to mind your own business," Holden fumed.

"Or what, Holden?"

Holden's face was contorted by the grip of his rage. "Maybe it's time you learn some manners."

"Maybe it is," Matt acknowledged. "But I don't think you're the man to teach me."

He looked easy and relaxed, but he was poised on the balls of his feet, and his hands were bunched. If Holden pushed it all the way, this could be a bad thing regardless of how it turned out. It would set the whole town to talking about it, and it was bound to get back to Holly. What would she think about it? Matt winced inwardly, thinking of how something like this would lacerate her.

Holden was sizing him up, trying to make up his mind about something.

Matt knew he was foolish, waiting for Holden to work himself up to the point that he would lose his head. A man was always crazy to give the other man the first blow. But that move had to come from Holden.

Something changed Holden's mind. Maybe it was the sight of Duncan, waiting across the street.

Matt wanted to tell him that Duncan wouldn't interfere, and he held it. That would only be pushing Holden into it, and Matt really didn't want that. Not because of what you'd like, he told himself. Because of Holly.

But he still wouldn't retreat a step, he wouldn't give Holden a thing. "Make up your mind," he said.

It hung on the raw edge of a precipice, and the wrong move or word could plunge it over.

Holden stared past Matt, and something he saw over Matt's shoulder had a visible effect on him. Matt wanted to turn his head to see what it was. But a man didn't do a foolish thing like that, particularly when he faced a furious man.

"Norborne, I'm telling you," he said huskily. "Don't ever put your nose in my business again."

He whirled abruptly and went down the street, the dust puffing up in little clouds from the savage thrusts of his heels.

Matt watched him with speculative eyes. Holden had been close to violent action, and something had changed his mind.

He turned, and Lo Yen was standing there, some twenty yards away. Could it have been the sight of Lo Yen that had forced Holden to change his mind? Lo Yen's face was blank, but his eyes were burning pools of hatred.

He approached Matt and asked, "Was he causing Ts'ai trouble?"

"No," Matt said. Lo Yen was already worked up. There was no use adding to it. "He offered to help her, and Ts'ai didn't want it."

"It was more than that," Lo Yen said, and the blaze in his eyes didn't dim. "I talked with Ts'ai this morning. She is afraid of him. I saw the way he looked at her. A man, who looks like that doesn't mean a woman any good."

Holden probably didn't know of the relationship between Lo Yen and Ts'ai, but he had sensed real menace in Lo Yen.

Matt shook his head. "You're reading more into it than there was."

"Am I?" Lo Yen asked. "Then why was it necessary for you to interfere?"

Matt's laugh was forced, and Lo Yen must catch its false ring. "Not that at all, Lo Yen."

"You are not a liar," Lo Yen said. The note of his voice said, but this time, you were. "I saw both of you. He was a man possessed with a devil. I was sure you would hit him. But he saw something that changed his mind. I think it was because I was here. I have seen other men look at her like that." Lo Yen could not be talked out of what he had seen and what he knew.

Lo Yen was right, but Matt could not admit it. Lo Yen had enough hating in him without adding fuel.

"Forget it, Lo Yen," he advised. "I'm promising you that he will not trouble you again."

"I know that," Lo Yen said simply. "If he ever tries it again, he will regret it."

"Good God," Matt said in exasperation. "If you so much as touch him, don't you know what would happen to you? White men would put a rope around your neck and hang you."

Lo Yen knew the truth of Matt's statement. But he could not be turned from an idea lodged in his head. "He will not trouble her again," he said stubbornly.

Matt put an arm across his shoulders. "I'm going to be around town for a couple more days. I'll keep an eye on her. I promise you that."

Lo Yen bobbed his head in grateful appreciation. But it wasn't enough. His implacable expression said that.

Matt waited for Duncan to cross the street and join them. He would have to gloss over the explanation Duncan would want. Going over it again would only harden Lo Yen's

69

determination. Lo Yen would take most orders Matt gave him but not in this. Matt's promise might satisfy him for the next few days. But what would happen after Matt was gone? He knew both of them were thinking about that.

CHAPTER ELEVEN

Matt moved his wagons outside of town and set up his camp there. It was cheaper buying groceries and preparing food for himself than eating meals in town. As far as sleeping on the ground that was no hardship. He would say that most of his nights had been slept that way.

He had spent that day, watching the Imler house, and he didn't see Ts'ai again. What he had been doing was probably foolish, but he had promised Lo Yen.

Duncan lay on his blankets and looked up at the stars. "This is probably a cleaner way for a man to spend his nights, but it sure isn't as much fun."

Matt laughed. "But think how you'll feel in the morning."

"I am," Duncan grumbled. "But I can't get much solace out of it. I guess I'm a bright light boy." He rolled over onto his side and propped his head up on his elbow. "Did you see Ts'ai or Holden today?"

Matt grinned. "Just Holden. I passed him once. The way he looked at me gave me the feeling he doesn't like me."

That pulled a laugh out of Duncan. "Maybe he's joined a select group."

"It's possible," Matt grunted. He had never gone out of his way to make an enemy, but he had never taken a backward step, either.

"Do you suppose he was back of Kung's killing?" Duncan asked suddenly.

The new thought hit Matt hard. "What makes you ask that?"

"It was a sure way of getting rid of Kung," Duncan said logically. "It left him a wide-open road to Ts'ai until you stepped in and blocked it."

71

"Yes," Matt admitted. It didn't mean he was accepting Duncan's idea, but it certainly opened a new viewpoint. He turned it over for a long moment but came to no conclusion. He would have to have too many questions answered before he could come up with any kind of an answer. How long had Holden known Ts'ai? When he had seen her for the first time would be the most important answer. He wished he could talk to Imler and Holly about it, but he knew he couldn't. Not without bringing cruel hurt to Holly.

Duncan thought his silence denoted disagreement, and he said, "Just the same, I'd keep an eye on him."

"Don't think I won't," Matt said savagely. He was almost angry at Duncan for bringing it up. Now he couldn't go to sleep. He couldn't get Holly Imler out of his mind. No matter how this turned out, she was bound to be hurt.

He turned and tossed, hearing Duncan's snoring deepen. Duncan was a lucky man not to burden his head with complex problems. Matt wished he could quit thinking of Holly. The moon climbed higher, and he was still awake. He would regret this lost sleep in the morning.

The smell of coffee and frying bacon awakened him. Duncan had breakfast going. "You don't look much better than if we had spent last night in town."

"I guess not," Matt said shortly. "You know that we can't spend more then another day in town. I'm not sure when the next load of pipe will reach Belleville, but we have to be there. We're beginning to lose the race against time and money."

Still, he wasted most of the day, doing nothing. He wished he knew where Holden was. He wasn't even sure that the man was still in town.

He saw Holly leave the house in the afternoon and was tempted to go in and talk to Imler. But what could Matt tell him that he could prove?

He wished he could tell Holly what he felt. How did a man go about telling a woman that her man was no good. He could see the shock in her eyes as he blurted it out. She wouldn't believe him, either. He was caught with something that he knew but couldn't prove. He wished he had some overt move of Holden's that he could nail him with.

Ts'ai came out an hour later, and Matt kept well behind her as she walked into town. She disappeared into a store, and Matt waited across the street. He swore at himself, at her, at the whole ridiculous involvement.

His face tightened as Holden came down the street. Had Holden seen her go into the store? Maybe not, but Holden's presence wasn't mere coincidence.

But Holden stopped before the store. Matt's jaw jutted. Holden had seen Ts'ai go into it. If Holden followed her, Matt was going in after him. After that, he would let events take their natural course. He was certain of one thing; if Holden bothered Ts'ai again, Matt was going to knock some sense into his head.

Holden started to open the door, then looked all around him. For an instant, Matt thought Holden didn't see him, then Holden's eyes came back to him.

He saw rage wash Holden's face as he stared at Matt, then he turned abruptly from the door. Matt hadn't built up something out of his imagination. Holden was obsessed with a drive, and nothing had changed him, yet.

Holden strode away, his anger showing in the long steps he took.

Matt checked himself from following him. He could force this until Holden lost his head. But what would that accomplish? Holden was an influential man, and he could make Matt look ridiculous. It would be his word against Matt's, and Matt knew where that would leave him.

He waited until Ts'ai came out, then crossed the street to join her. He smiled at her and said, "Let me help you." He took the packages from her arms.

She thanked him with her eyes, but a heavy shadow was in them. "He was here?" she asked.

73

He could lie to her, and she would not believe him. "Yes," he said gravely.

She drew a deep breath. "I am afraid of him."

Matt swore under his breath. "Have you talked to the Imlers about this?"

"What could I say to them? That a foolish woman is ridden by her fears? Would they believe me? I cannot hurt Miss Holly."

Matt groaned inwardly. That was the obstacle both of them faced.

"I do not think he will leave me alone," she said with a half sob.

He tried to soothe her, and his words sounded hollow, even to himself. He guessed he was going to have to knock Holden's head off.

He left her at Imler's door. "If it gets too bad, will you promise me one thing; promise me that you'll talk to Mr. Imler about it."

He wasn't satisfied with her reluctant assent, but he could do no better at the moment. He turned away from the door, and Lo Yen was coming toward him. The man moved like a shadow; at one moment, there was nothing; the next, he was here.

He didn't have to ask Lo Yen, if he had seen it. It was written in those furious eyes.

"He will not leave her alone," Lo Yen said savagely.

That made two of them Matt had to be concerned about. "Lo Yen, your sister promised me that she would say something to Imler, if he molests her again. I don't think Imler would stand for it."

That didn't appease Lo Yen, for he stubbornly shook his head. "I will watch her."

"We can't spend all of our time just keeping an eye on her," Matt said wearily. "We've got to get back to camp tomorrow. I expect pipe in Belleville the day after or the next."

"I am not going," Lo Yen said flatly.

74

Dismay flooded Matt's face. "You can't stay here. I can't talk to the men, if you're not there."

"You will not need them to go after the pipe." There was no giving in Lo Yen's words.

"I guess not," Matt said reluctantly. "Duncan and I planned to go after it."

"I will stay here a few more days." Resentment flooded Lo Yen's face as he thought he saw refusal in Matt's eyes. "Can you think of something better?"

"No," Matt confessed. He saw that he couldn't budge Lo Yen, and he didn't blame the man. "All right," he acknowledged. "Maybe Holden will change his mind when he sees that you're always around." It wasn't satisfactory to him, and he warned, "Don't lay hands on him, Lo Yen. I told you what that could bring. If Holden tries to approach her again, go to Dent Imler. He'll listen to you." He prayed to God that Imler would.

CHAPTER TWELVE

Holden restlessly paced his room. The thought of Ts'ai was driving him crazy. He had tried to get her out of his head and couldn't. Every place he looked he saw her face. He cursed himself again for being caught up in something he couldn't control. He was risking losing Holly, and that no longer seemed to matter. He knew how she would react with the first word she caught of this. That didn't deter him. If he only had the opportunity to talk to Ts'ai without Norborne interfering. He could make Ts'ai listen to him; he was certain of that. Money was the answer to everything. He could offer her advantages she never dreamed of.

He looked at his flushed reflection in the mirror. If he could only talk to her without that damned watchdog Norborne being around. Norborne must be interested in her, too. The thought pounded at him. Goddamn him! He should have hired Steiger to put a bullet in Norborne. His lips pulled back in a snarl. It was too late to think of that now.

He sat down behind his desk, then bounced up again. He couldn't sit still. Where was that Hai Ling? He had never seen the man, but he had heard that he was one of the leaders of the Chinese element in Candelaria. Holden wanted to talk to him. He had left word in Candelaria yesterday that he wanted to see him him early this morning. It was after nine o'clock. If this was an example of Chinese reliability, it only confirmed his opinion of them.

He cursed the silence of the mill. That, upon everything else, unnerved him. Without the pound of the stamps, he was lost. His temper had put him in a bind. He shouldn't have fired Sadler and the others until he was certain about getting replacements for them.

He turned his head at the knock on the door. It was light as though it had timidity behind it. "Come in," he growled.

He was behind his desk again when the Chinese came into the room. The size of the man surprised him. He was a hulking brute, much larger than the average Chinese. If he did hire the man, he could expect to get a little honest work out of him.

"You Hai Ling?"

The deference in Hai Ling's nod pleased Holden. The man knew his place, and that was a good start. "You took long enough to get here."

"I walked from Candelaria," the man said quietly.

That was no suitable explanation. Why didn't the man ride? If he didn't have a horse, he could have ridden over on one of the ore wagons. The thought struck Holden that the ore wagons weren't running now. He pushed it aside. It still didn't excuse Hai Ling. A more reliable man could have gotten a ride from some source.

"I'm thinking of hiring Chinese in my mill. Have you had any experience?"

The question unleashed a torrent of words from Hai Ling. He spoke passable English, and that was good. Holden wouldn't have to try to understand that heathenish gibberish the others spoke.

"I have," Hai Ling said. "I worked in mills at the Comstock." His pock-marked face was suddenly animated, and that could be nothing but hope lighting his eyes. "But it had been a long time since I have worked."

He was a hungry man, Holden thought. That also was good. A hungry man could be so much more easily handled.

"Why haven't you worked? Haven't you looked for it?"

"Ever since I came to Candelaria. I could find a day here, a day there. But nothing steady. It is hard for a Chinese to find work—" He shrugged with a fatalistic acceptance that said it all.

It was a weak excuse, Holden thought contemptuously. If a man wanted work badly enough, he could get it. "I'll pay a dollar seventy-five cents a day."

Hai Ling threw out his hands. "But that is half of what—" He stopped, deciding that sounded wrong. "Even Norborne pays the Chinese he hires more than that."

The name brought a flash of fire into Holden's eyes. "Then go to work for him," he snapped.

"I tried." That was defeat in Hai Ling's manner. "Even as late as yesterday. He has no more jobs." His voice was low as though he talked to only himself. "I thought there might be. After Kung was murdered."

Holden drew in a careful breath. "How do you know that?"

Hai Ling shrugged. "I have heard talk about it. That is all."

"When did you talk to Norborne?" Holden went back over his contact with Steiger. Did Norborne know something more about it?

"Yesterday," Hai Ling repeated. "He said he was leaving this morning to go back to his pipeline."

Holden kept the elation from showing in his face. He had no reason to doubt Hai Ling's words. Norborne was gone, and excitement stole along Holden's veins. Hai Ling could be useful to him in more ways than one.

"Maybe I can raise the wage to two dollars a day."

He saw the gratitude fill Hai Ling's eyes, and his contempt grew. All that for a measly quarter more a day.

"Can you find me about twenty more men, men who have worked in a mill?"

"Yes, yes," Hai Ling said eagerly. "I can find them. I will have them here tomorrow. I go now to begin."

Holden checked him. "By the way, do you know a woman called Ts'ai. She works in Dent Imler's house."

Was that a wariness stealing across the man's face? If he denied it, Holden would boot him.

"I know her," Hai Ling said cautiously. "Ts'ai Kung.

78

She is the widow of the man who was killed. He did not ask why, but his attitude did.

"I want to talk to her. I want to hire her away from Imler." He chuckled with elaborate ease. "I'm tired of listening to Imler boast how good she is. But I cannot go to his house and hire her under his nose, can I?"

Hai Ling brightened. He had seen the rivalry between white men before, and it took strange forms.

"You can talk to her," he said. "Early each morning, she takes her son to leave at her aunt's house." He described where it was, and Holden nodded. He could find it.

"But it is too late this morning," Hai Ling said regretfully.

"In the morning, then," Holden said carelessly. "I don't want you saying anything about this. It could get back to Imler."

Hai Ling vigorously shook his head. "I tell no one." This belonged in the white man's business. He had learned that the more he stayed out of it, the better off he was.

He beamed broadly. The gods of fortune had smiled on him today. "I will have them here in the morning."

"Make it at noon," Holden said. "That will be soon enough."

He waited until the door closed, then smashed his fist into his palm. My God, how this day had turned out from its beginning. He had hired a work force for about half of what he had been paying, and best of all, he would talk to Ts'ai in the morning.

He sat in his buggy a half block down from the house Hai Ling had described. It was early, and the town wasn't yet fully stirring. He fretted impatiently. He preferred that as few people as possible see him. Damn her, he thought in quick anger. What was keeping her so long?

He saw her coming down the street, and by the way she hurried, she must be late. She looked neither to the right nor left as she entered the house. A baby, he thought in

79

quick disgust at himself. And he had even thought of offering marriage. A man's desires could drive him into the craziest of decisions.

He started the mare and moved the buggy before the door. He could see where the baby would work to his advantage. She was a widow, and the baby only meant that money would be that much more important to her.

Good God, what was keeping her now? He kept looking up and down the street. It remained empty, but he couldn't depend upon that too long. If he was seen with her, how tongues would wag. That would surely get back to the Imlers. If she only came out now, he could avoid all that. He could still keep his hold on Holly. He gloated over his cleverness. He could still have both of them.

He sighed in relief as she shut the door behind her. "Ts'ai," he called. "Over here."

That was fright on her face as she flung up her head. She looked all around, and for an instant, he thought she would flee.

"Come here," he snapped. "It's important."

She came reluctantly toward the buggy, and he extended a hand. "Holly has hurt herself. She is asking for you."

Her expressive face mirrored various emotions. "Is it true?"

He put a wheedling smile on his face. "Don't you believe me, Ts'ai? It is true. Holly isn't badly hurt, but she is asking for you."

"I walk," Ts'ai said in sudden decision.

Holden looked reproachful. Inwardly, he wanted to grab her and shake some sense into her head. "And have her wait that much longer? I thought you cared for her more than that."

"I do, I do," Ts'ai cried in quick distress. "I go with you."

She climbed into the buggy, and he made no attempt to touch her. Her instinctive fear of him was swallowed up by a greater emergency.

She sat as far away from him as she could. "How did it happen? She is not hurt bad?"

Holden snapped the reins on the mare's rump. "I told you that, didn't I?" Everything was going his way. As far as he could tell not a person had seen him pick her up, and in a few more moments he would be out of town.

"This is not the way," she cried in quick alarm.

"A better way," he assured her. "And easier on the mare." If she understood that, it didn't loosen her face.

He passed old man Fairfield's shack at the edge of town. Fairfield had died a year ago, and nobody had wanted this miserable hovel.

"This is not the way," she insisted. "Where are you taking me?"

He thought the little fool was going to jump out, and he reached over and gripped her wrist. She struggled against his hold, and he said harshly, "Stop it. I only want to talk to you."

She pulled as far away as she could from him, and he thought she was going to make another attempt to jump. "You do," he threatened, "and you'll break your arm."

He heard her quicker breathing, sounding almost like sobs. That wouldn't last long. He had a certain way to quiet her down.

He pulled up a mile out of town but didn't let go of her wrist. "Why are you afraid of me, Ts'ai?"

"I'm not," she denied. She tried to look at him, and she couldn't hold it. "But why did you lie to me?"

His laugh was an easy thing; it all was coming his way now. "Just so I could talk to you. Would you have talked to me at the Imlers' house, or any place else? I tried a couple of times before."

She slowly shook her head. "Because I was afraid," she whispered. "I know why you looked at me like that. I did not want Miss Holly ever to see it."

Her fear wasn't because of him but because of Holly, and he expanded with the knowledge. She had all the instincts of a woman. She would not let go of what she had in hand until she had something better. It made everything for him so much easier.

"I don't want her to know either, Ts'ai. Why does she have to know?"

She gave him the full impact of her eyes for a long moment, then dropped them. Holden could appreciate that. That was the only a woman's normal reaction. Now was the time to make her look at him again, and this time, she would not look away.

He still held her wrist as a precaution, and with the other hand he pulled a pack of bills from his coat pocket. He placed them in her lap, and he knew how her face would change when she learned how much was there. A hundred dollars was in that packet, and he had no doubt it was more money than she had ever seen at one time in her life.

"A hundred dollars, Ts'ai," he said softly. "Think of everything it will do for you. Think of what it will do for your son."

She tugged gently at her wrist, and he released it. He wanted to laugh aloud. Her eyes were riveted on the money, and its hypnotic force was reflected in her face.

"It is so much money," she whispered.

Now she would listen to him. "There's more where that came from. For anything you want. You don't have to be the Imlers' servant any more."

He leaned toward her, his mouth seeking her lips. She pushed at him with both hands with surprising force and quickness. It shoved him off balance, and she sprang out of the buggy.

He stared dumbly at the bills spilled out of her lap and onto the floor. An errant wind picked up a few of them and carried them away. The unexpectedness of it stunned him, and for a moment, he was anchored to the seat.

His face flushed, and his eyes were wild. The little bitch had tricked him. She had led him along, and he had followed her like a naïve fool.

She was in full flight, and he roared at her. "Come back here."

If she heard him, she didn't turn her head. But it spurred her on with a new urgency.

He jumped to the ground and ran after her, and the madness in him demanded he catch and punish her. She would find out what her trickery got her.

He hadn't thought a woman could run this fast, and for a long moment, he was sure he was losing ground to her. Then he began to gain. She should have known that his longer stride and greater stamina were more than any woman could equal.

She turned her head, and he was close enough to see the despair flood her face. He could hear the sobbing, tearing sound of her breathing, and she tried too hard, or stepped into a depression, for she fell.

Her fall pulled a triumphant yell from him. He expected to see her crumple in a helpless heap, but she still had a small, additional effort left. She tried to crawl along the ground, and it gave him a cruel amusement to think that she looked like a wounded animal, trying to reach some hole of concealment.

His face was livid when he caught up with her. He was tempted to kick the life out of her, and he restrained it. That would come later, but first, she had to know how stupid she was.

"You little deceiving bitch," he raged. "I offered you anything you wanted. But you were too blind to see it."

Tears streaked her dust-smeared face. He stared at her in disbelief. How could this woman have had such a tremendous attraction for him?

Her face was distorted with fear as she looked up at him. "Please. I did not harm you."

Ah, but she had. He reached down, seized her by the shoulder, and yanked her to her feet.

She hung in his hands like a limp doll, crying in uncontrollable gasps. He pulled her to him, seeking her mouth. She would remember this but not for long.

83

She jerked her face from him, but her resistance was only a feeble token.

"You little fool," he said before his mouth closed on hers.

"Let go of her," a voice behind him said.

Its shocking impact froze his muscles. He hadn't even realized that anybody was near. He let go of her and whipped his head around. Lo Yen and two other Chinese stood there, all of them panting as though they had just finished a hard run.

The implacable cast of their faces chilled him to the bone. He cursed himself for not putting that .38 in his pocket. But how could he guess that he would need a gun?

He held up his hands, palms outward, and retreated a few steps. If only he could get to the buggy, he would be all right, but they were between it and him. They followed him, fanning out in a half circle, and the look on their faces dried his mouth and left his tongue as stiff and unyielding as a piece of wood.

CHAPTER THIRTEEN

His hands were still held up against them. "Wait," he pleaded. "You don't understand."

Ts'ai's crying was muted, and he glanced at her. Her hands covered her face, and he wanted to beg her to intercede. He stopped the useless words before they were formed.

"Go home, Ts'ai," Lo Yen said. "Don't talk to anybody about this."

Her lips trembled as she looked at him. "I will not talk." Part of the emotion in her voice could have been shame. She broke into a run, and her steps were weak.

Lo Yen's mirthless grin was only a brief pulling back of his lips. "You could not let her alone, could you?"

Holden's lips trembled in an ashen face. "I didn't mean her any harm. I was only trying to talk to her."

That mean grin was fixed on Lo Yen's mouth. "Bad talk to make her cry and fear you?" He said a sharp word in Chinese to the other two.

They came at him like three enraged animals, and Holden fought them off with all the frantic strength in his being. With his size he could have handled one of them, or perhaps even two, but the third made the difference. Each time he knocked one of them down, or threw him off, the other two attacked him from a new angle.

They did not know how to use their fists well. They clawed at him with nails, butted him with their heads, and kicked at him. He felt the sharp stinging of the lacerations they traced on his face, and his lungs were on fire with the relentless demand he put on them. He felt his coat rip down the back, and a sleeve was torn away.

His first fear was that they would use knives on him, or

worse, a gun, but they didn't. They kept him backing up, and each step carried him farther from the buggy.

He had marked them. He could see color coming into the bruises on their faces. My God, he thought frantically, won't anything stop them? He dared risk a glance about him, hoping to see a club, a rock, a weapon of any kind.

That cost him. Lo Yen sprang on him again, and his arms wrapped about his neck. He pulled at the arms that were choking him, and the fear was rising in him. It lodged in his throat, draining the strength from his muscles. Nothing would stop them.

He ducked and threw Lo Yen off, and two more were on him.

He made the serious mistake of trying to cope with them all at once, instead of trying to finish one of them at a time. By the time he had decided that, his strength was definitely ebbing.

His sobbing rattled in his throat. They intended to kill him, and he almost wished they had a faster way.

One of them kicked his legs out from under him, and he went down smothered by all of their weight.

He heaved up, throwing one of them off, and Lo Yen slammed an elbow into his face. The darkness hovered over him, and he prayed it move in and take him. Anything would be better than this mounting total of hurts and bruises. His lungs were on fire, and his vision was impaired. He quit all at once, lying on his back in the dust, whimpering like a baby.

Another blow thudded into his face, and it made his whimpering louder.

Lo Yen checked the other two. "It is enough," he said, panting against his pumping lungs.

The smallest one of them looked at Holden, spat out a mouthful of blood, and said, "The white man doesn't fight so well."

Lo Yen's eyes were fastened onto the quivering mass on

the ground, and they showed no pity. "Not with one of them against three of us," he said sardonically.

Holden showed the marks of the cruel beating. His face was crisscrossed with scratches, and one of his eyes was completely shut. Saliva kept forming at his mouth, then bursting in little, red bubbles. He was barely conscious, and his clothing was a complete ruin. It would be a long time before he could walk with ease.

"It is not enough," the second one said angrily. "We should have killed him."

Lo Yen remembered the warning Matt had given him and shook his head. "No, cousin. If he ever looks at a Chinese woman again, this will come back to him. If we did more, then for sure they would hang us."

"You think they won't now," Sun Yat-sen said fiercely. "He will tell, and they will be looking for us."

Lo Yen debated that and again shook his head. "I do not think so. His pride will prevent it. Besides, I think I am the only one he knows. I have heard the white man say, one Chinese cannot be told from another."

It did not suit them, and they grumbled.

Lo Yen motioned at Holden. "There he is. Finish him. It would take small effort."

They glanced at each other, and their grumbling stopped. Something held them. It could have been the helpless, inanimate, bloody mass, or perhaps it was the threat of the hanging.

"I guess not," Sun Yat-sen said. "It is as you say. He has enough to remember it."

He wriggled a loose tooth as he looked at the horse and buggy. "Do we take it with us?"

"We are not thieves," Lo Yen said with dignity.

Holden did not know how long he lay on the ground. He stirred, and the movement put new life into each hurt and ache. He groaned against it and shut his good eye. The sun had climbed quite a way, and its fierce rays were small, additional clubs, beating at him.

He tried to sit up and groaned as he couldn't make it. God, wasn't anybody going to help him?

He lay back, waiting for renewed strength to flow back into him. His head threatened to pound itself off of his shoulders, and his thoughts were fragmented and hazy. It came back a small piece at a time. When he came to, he had the fuzzy impression that he had been in some kind of accident. But that wasn't right at all. The Chinese had waylaid him and beat him. It uncapped a new fountain of fury, and he cursed them until his voice was weak. The goddamned Chinese; how he hated every one of them. He wished they were lined up before him, and he had enough ammunition to shoot down every one of them. He would gladly spend the rest of his life in doing nothing else. That included Ts'ai. Her treachery had started all of this.

He let go of such useless thoughts. He could do nothing about the Chinese, and that included her and the other three. He couldn't without his part in this coming out. He could not stand the thought of being the laughingstock of the town.

He struggled to a sitting position, and the effort drained him. He sat with his elbows propped on his knees, his head cradled in his hands. God, how he hurt. His nose started bleeding again, and he watched the slow fall of the red drops. God, how he hated Ts'ai and the others. "It's not over yet," he muttered in a cracked voice. "I'll even it some way."

Matt Norborne! The name flashed into his mind. Norborne was behind all this. He had put the Chinese up to attacking him. He cursed Norborne until he could make no more sound. Norborne had a special place in his hating, too.

He could not sit here all day, even though he knew the anguish new movement would cost him. If he could just get to his buggy— A new fear split his head. What if it wasn't here; what if those thieving Chinese had taken it? He looked in the direction where he had left it, and the fear increased, savagely raking him. He couldn't see it. The rasp of his breathing increased until it was almost a sobbing. How could he get back to town without it?

He cried aloud in relief. He couldn't plainly make it out, but it was there, a darker mass against the sand. But it seemed so far away. Had the fighting carried him this distance?

He tried to stand and couldn't make it. He gritted his teeth and tried again. He could not wait until somebody happened along and saw him.

He could make it to his hands and knees and remained there, his head hanging low. He started crawling, a painful, slow progress. A dozen times he knew he had to quit, and he forced himself on.

He could make out the details of the buggy, and the mare was getting restless at the apparition approaching her. The nervous mincing of her forehoofs drove him crazy. What would he do, if she broke on him? He wanted to rave at her, and he knew he had to keep his voice low and even.

"Easy, Lady," he said. "Easy, girl."

Whether or not she recognized him, or a familiar voice reached her he didn't know. But she held.

He reached out and grabbed a spoke of the rear wheel and dragged himself to his feet. He leaned against its support before he could make the supreme effort of hauling himself into the buggy.

He made it and sprawled across the seat. The mare was dancing again, her ears flicking back and forth, but it didn't matter now; he had the reins in his hands.

He sat up, feeling stronger. He saw the smear of dirt and blood on the red-leather seat, and made no visible sign, though the rage was coursing through him again. He had been so proud of the buggy.

He started the mare at a slow pace, and it seemed as though he could feel every pebble, every obstacle in the road. He supposed he should see a doctor, but he couldn't do that. That would open the barrage of questions that he couldn't face.

He would give anything for a drink of water, but he hadn't brought a canteen along. That was like the .38; how would he have thought it would be so needed before this morning was over?

He increased the pace; he had to get back to his office. He would find water there, and he could soothe the stinging of his face and hands.

He drove around Candelaria and didn't pass anybody until he was halfway up the ridge that separated the two towns. A freighter passed and hailed him with an upraised hand. Holden turned his head away. He recognized the man; he hoped the man couldn't say the same of him. The freight wagon had been going at a faster clip on the descent, and already it was a hundred yards away. He might have recognized Holden by the buggy, but Holden was sure he couldn't have seen the shape he was in.

He came into Columbus from the back way and left the mare and buggy outside of his office door. He was fearful that somebody, in the mill, would see him, then he remembered no one was there any more.

He had stiffened up during the drive here, and he groaned at the agony of getting down and climbing the stairs. He entered his office, closed the door, and leaned against it, too spent to cross immediately to the water pitcher. He had made it; he had beaten those damned Chinks. They had thought he couldn't do it, for he was quite sure they thought him dead or dying when they left him.

He limped across the room and lifted the pitcher. He remembered to take off his hat, and it wasn't on his head. He had lost it some place, and he hadn't even thought to look for it.

He let the water run over his bowed head, choking back the yelps he wanted to make against its stinging touch. It ran down his face and neck, puddling on the floor, and he didn't care.

90

He raised the pitcher again and drank the remaining water. It ran off his chin and down his shirt front. He felt immensely better when he set the pitcher down. For the first time, he could honestly think he was going to live. He forced himself to walk over to the mirror. He said a weak "Jesus" as he looked at his reflection. He could not believe what he saw. His face was swollen and discolored, and the water hadn't been enough to remove all of the caked blood. His mouth was puffy too, and he had a momentary fear for his teeth. He bared them and knew a tremendous relief. There were no gaps in them. He remembered at least once, that he had been kicked in the face. That could have easily knocked out a tooth, or several of them.

He swore in a dull monotone as he surveyed the damage. His clothing was completely ruined, even his shirt and pants.

Swearing dripped steadily from his mouth as he recalled how much that new suit had cost him. He looked at himself in the mirror again. It would be several days before he could appear looking like this, and his facile mind searched for a plausible explanation in case somebody asked about it. He had been waylaid by a band of footpads and was lucky enough to fight his way clear. He nodded with satisfaction. Nobody would try to dispute Gary Holden's word.

He had another change of clothes in the office, and he stripped off the ruined ones. He grimaced at each new bruise he saw. He must have been kicked repeatedly after he was semiconscious. He could take a small pride in one thing. It took a good man to survive a beating like he had taken.

He had barely finished dressing when he heard a knock on the door. He threw a startled look at it. Who could that be?

"It is Hai Ling," a voice said. "I have returned like I told you I would."

For a moment, Holden couldn't breathe as a new fury gripped his throat. That stupid bastard. He had the gall to show up here after what had happened. But Hai Ling could

91

not possibly know. Holden swept the rational thought aside. That made no difference; he would not excuse him for that.

As he limped to the door, he heard voices speaking that heathenish gibberish. He threw it open, and Hai Ling's mouth sagged. More Chinese were bunched behind him.

"You have been in an accident," he gasped.

Holden cursed them with every oath at his command. "Get out of here," he screamed. "I wouldn't have one of you damned Chinks around, if you worked for nothing."

Consternation loosened Hai Ling's face, and the others looked as equally stunned. "But you told me—"

"Goddamn you!" Holden raved. "Can't you understand plain English? I told you to get out of here."

He whirled and limped as fast as he could go. He pulled out the desk drawer, and shock still had them rooted.

His hand came into view with the .38, and they broke and ran. He fired at Hai Ling and saw the man duck. They scattered like a bunch of frightened chickens, and he heard their footsteps pounding down the hallway. Even though he could not see any of them he fired again. He ran to the doorway, and the last man was disappearing down the steps. He fired at him and frustration made him want to cry. He missed again.

CHAPTER FOURTEEN

Duncan rolled his shoulders to ease the creeping ache in them.

He was doing that more frequently, and Matt jeered, "Are you getting soft?"

"You want to trade?" Duncan growled. He didn't take his eyes off of the menacing mountains around them. They were so vast, and a hundred alert men couldn't cover all the spots where a skulking ambusher might hide. Both he and Matt knew that. Luck had to be with them, if somebody was out to get them. All Duncan could depend upon was a flash of movement, an unnaturalness about a place that might draw his attention before the ambusher fired.

Matt grinned. "I'm content where I am." Both the driver of the wagon and the guard knew the same strain. Duncan hadn't laid down the rifle since they had started, and Matt could feel the tension of holding the reins, knotting the muscles in his forearms.

Duncan sighed. "If a man only knew where it was coming from with a couple of seconds to act first."

Matt shook his head but not in denial. Duncan's complaint was justified. The waiting for something to happen and not even knowing it was going to could tie up a man. The wagon was empty, and he didn't think an attack, if one was coming, would come on this half of the trip. But still, he couldn't afford to relax. He couldn't stand the loss of another wagon, plus the team. And that wasn't counting his and Duncan's hides. Coming back loaded would be an entirely different matter. Then the strain would really sit in.

He let the teams plod at their own pace. The worst crossing

of the mountains was behind them, and the downward slope was now in their favor.

"I just hope that damned pipe is there," he fretted.

Duncan nodded in sympathy. He could echo that hope. They rode the rest of the way in silence. They passed the end of rail a few miles out of Belleville. The Carson & Colorado Railroad was pushing track hard. Matt paused a moment to watch a gang of Chinese workmen. They worked together like the well-engineered parts of a smoothly running machine. The tong men would snake a rail off a flat car, carry it a few yards ahead to where the track ended and lower it in place on the already laid ties. Up ahead, other gangs dropped ties in place on the well-packed bed, or at least, all the packing it was going to get. The rail no sooner was on the ties when the spike men went to work, the rhythmic pounding of their hammers only ceasing when the spikes were driven. They were chanting something that had to be a Chinese song.

"They're good workers," Matt said soberly. "They work for a hell of a lot less than a white man would take."

"Would you?" Duncan asked.

"No," Matt said flatly. But a white man would work far harder and for almost nothing, if the project was his. Maybe that characteristic was the force driving this country ahead.

Matt picked up the reins. "Let's go see how lucky we are."

Belleville was a motley collection of shacks, hovels, and patched tents. A few enterprising men had filled empty whiskey cases with dirt, then stacked them like bricks to make the walls of their dwelling. The lettering of the original shippers were still plain on them.

The railhead had made Belleview grow like a toadstool. Matt wouldn't begin to estimate how much the population had increased. Overnight, it sprang into roaring life, and with the fragility of a toadstool, it would shrivel almost as fast as it had grown after the track had moved on.

Matt drove to the temporary freight office. He crossed two fingers at Duncan, and the gesture prayed that the shipment was on time. The railroad supplies would always come through first.

"Me, too," Duncan agreed and slumped in the seat. He hadn't relaxed all the way here.

Matt walked into the part building, part tent, and the ending of the day's heat hammered on the canvas roof. A harried clerk worked behind a counter that was overloaded with paper work. A job like that would drive Matt crazy. The confinement was bad enough, but this man worked against an increasing avalanche of paper work that threatened to engulf him.

"Norborne," Matt said. "Did my shipment of pipe get through?"

For a moment, he thought the thin-faced, prematurely balding man would blow up at him for the interruption, then he caught himself.

"Let me check, Mr. Norborne."

Matt didn't smile, though he wanted to. The clerk had a better hold on himself than Matt would have had.

The clerk went through paper after paper, leaving one pile to thumb through another. Matt fidgeted, and he could feel the sweat trickling down from his armpits. More than just heat was behind the sweating. What if his shipment had been lost, or delayed? He looked at the hopeless mass of paper. How in the hell could a man find the exact piece in that?

"Here it is." The clerk looked up, and his face brightened. Finding it was a minor triumph, and Matt doubted that the man had opportunity for bigger triumphs.

"You'll find it on a spur just south of town," the clerk said. "It's all yours."

Matt grinned. It should be. He had paid for the complete purchase of pipe in San Francisco, asking for spaced shipments so that he could cut down his handling of it. If it had all been delivered at once, he would have to reload a lot of it as the line advanced. It had worked well until he had lost that load.

95

"Sign here, Mr. Norborne." The clerk turned the paper around. "Next week, you won't have to drive quite so far. One of these days, we'll be clear to Candelaria."

Matt nodded as he scribbled his name. Right now, he wished the railroad was already there. That would not only cut down the distance, it would eliminate that long haul through the mountains.

"I'll see you again," he said as he tucked his copy of the shipment into his pocket.

He looked back from the door. The clerk had already started burrowing again in the paper work.

"It's here, Riley," he said before he climbed into the wagon. "We've still got enough daylight to load it. That will give us an early start in the morning."

Duncan groaned at the thought of the labor that would demand from two men. It would take both of them to handle one of those two-inch, twenty-one foot length of pipe, and they wouldn't toss it around as though it was a matchstick.

Matt had no difficulty in finding the spur. He stopped before the pile of pipe, and with nothing to confine it, it had sprawled over quite an area. Round pipe was impossible to stack unless it had something like wagon sides to hold it.

Duncan looked at it sourly. "Looks like they doubled our shipment. Hell, we can't get all of that in one wagon."

"We can try," Matt said cheerfully. How he wished it was an overshipment. He would gladly come back the day after tomorrow for whatever was left.

Darkness was falling fast as the last length was loaded and the load chained to prevent from shifting.

"All we've got to do is to get it back," Matt said.

He unharnessed the leading team, while Duncan took the second one. The horses had to be fed and staked out for the night.

"Feel like finding out what the town has to offer tonight?" he asked.

Duncan considered it before he shook his head. "I'm too

damned tired. I don't want you shaking me awake in the morning without me being able to get my eyes open."

That suited Matt fine as he began preparing their own meal, prior to bedding down for the night.

In the morning Matt harnessed the teams while Duncan cooked breakfast. Bacon and coffee and bread that had been baked too long ago made a skimpy breakfast.

Matt scoured the tin plates with sand, kicked more of it over the dying embers of the fire and asked, "Ready to roll?"

Duncan heaved himself up to the seat. "As ready as I'll ever be." He had a tight grip on the rifle.

With the heavy load the teams barely crawled up the grade. It wouldn't be a difficult target for an ambusher. The slow-moving wagon was little more than stationary.

As the morning wore on they exchanged no light talk. Duncan was too busy probing every shadow ahead and behind them, and the climbing turns demanded all of Matt's attention. He sighed as they reached the crest. We're going to make it. The thought was big in his mind, but he didn't dare put it into words. The descent was ahead of them.

He drew a deep breath as the wagon rumbled out onto the flat. He could ease off now. He saw the workers waiting for them at the campsite ahead, and he whacked Duncan on the shoulder. He could say it now.

"We made it, Riley. Whoever was after that first load wasn't interested in this one."

Ducan's face loosened. He held out his hand, and the finger was hooked. "I held that damned rifle so hard, I can't straighten my fingers."

Matt grinned before his face sobered. When tension left a man, it was like a big load rolling off of his back. He wished Lo Yen was here. It was going to be hard to handle those foreign-talking Chinese without Lo Yen being around.

His eyes widened as the wagon rolled close enough for him to make out individual faces. Lo Yen was here. Something had happened in Candelaria for Lo Yen to leave it this soon. Two Chinese stood beside Lo Yen, and to the best of Matt's knowledge he hadn't seen either of them before.

He stopped the wagon and handed the reins to Duncan. Duncan knew what to do with it. He would drive to where the pipe ended and get the Chinese busy laying out new lengths.

He jumped down, and the wagon pulled away. Lo Yen approached him, and his face was as inscrutable as ever, but something worked in his eyes. It could be concern and pleasure too, and it was an odd mixture. The two other Chinese were right behind him.

"What are you doing here?" Matt demanded. Not that he wasn't grateful. The work would go so much better with Lo Yen's presence. "I thought you were worried about Ts'ai."

"I was." The past tense was a strange way to put it. "I think that worry is over now."

The two Chinese looked at each other and grinned. Matt's eyes swept their faces. All of them had been in some kind of a brawl. The signs of it were on their faces. He looked back at Lo Yen. Had these three been fighting each other?

"You better tell me about it, Lo Yen."

Lo Yen bobbed his head. "I intended to. These are my cousins, Sun Yat-sen and Yang Yat-sen. They helped me."

"Helped you do what?" Matt asked. That pleasure seemed to have grown in Lo Yen's eyes.

Lo Yen ignored the question, at least, for the moment. "I told them it is possible you have work for them."

Matt's temper was rising. It wasn't like this for Lo Yen to be this evasive.

"You know I haven't, Lo Yen." That wasn't quite accurate. Kung's death left him a man short. But he was going to get along without hiring any more men, if he could.

"I was afraid of that," Lo Yen said gravely. "It is too bad. But they, like me, must stay out of Candelaria."

"Why?"

"For beating Holden. The three of us gave him a beating he will not forget for a long time."

Matt's jaw sagged. "Damnit, Lo Yen. Didn't I tell you what could happen, if you touched him?"

"And I remembered it. We did not kill him, though it was tempting. He got Ts'ai into his buggy by saying that Miss Holly was hurt, then driving her out of town." Wry amusement cracked that mask. "It was hard to catch up with a buggy when a man is on foot. It was a very hard run to reach him as quick as we did. Even then, his hands were on her. Ts'ai was very frightened."

Matt digested that, and it focused his anger on Holden. "That bastard! He's lucky I didn't catch him. I'd have broken his damned neck."

"And your reason would have been enough," Lo Yen said seriously.

Matt wanted to grin. Lo Yen took his words literally.

"Your warning did not stop Holden," Lo Yen went on. "When a man is driven, it is hard to keep a warning in his head." He filled in the details and finally said, "So you see, my cousins had to leave with me. Holden might not recognize us again, but we could not risk that."

"I'll find something for them here, Lo Yen. But who will watch Ts'ai now?"

Lo Yen said a few rapid Chinese words to his cousins. What he said must have been pleasing, for broad grins split their faces.

"I do not think it is necessary," Lo Yen said. "I do not think he will ever look at her again."

It wasn't enough for Matt. Somebody had to know what was going on. He thought of Dent Imler and scowled. Imler might refuse to believe him and order him out, but it was something he had to face. He groaned inwardly as he thought, Holly is bound to learn, too. He was sorry about that, but he could see no other course.

His face brightened. "Maybe Ts'ai will say something to Imler."

"I think not," Lo Yen said softly. "Would she want to be the one to hurt Miss Holly?"

"No," Matt agreed, and his face was brooding. "Ts'ai would not talk to Holly about this."

He made an abrupt decision. Imler had to be told about it. He writhed under the thought of what it would do to his standing with Dent Imler and Holly, but it couldn't be helped.

"Tell Duncan where I've gone," he said. "And for God's sake, will you see to it that a little pipe is laid."

Lo Yen kept bobbing his head, and his face was open and happy. "We will work very good. You will see."

Matt dismounted before the Imler house. He would rather take a physical beating than what he faced. He hoped that Imler was in and Holly wasn't. He swore softly. A man caught in a river like this couldn't pick its current.

He rapped on the door, running a dozen approaches over in his mind. He found no easy way, and he guessed he would just have to blurt it out.

He got a small break, for Dent Imler answered the door.

"Come in," Imler invited, and the invitation was cordial.

"Is Holly in?"

Curiosity flashed in Imler's eyes. "Why no, she isn't. She and Ts'ai went down town to do some shopping. They should be in any time."

So far, a minor part of Matt's luck was holding, but he still had to tell Imler.

He followed Imler into the parlor and turned down an offer of a glass of wine.

"I can make it stronger," Imler said.

Matt shook his head. This was no social visit, and fumbling around wouldn't solve anything.

"Is Ta'si all right?"

A small frown creased Imler's forehead. "Why shouldn't she be?"

Matt took a deep breath and dived in. "She had a rough experience. Holden manhandled her."

Imler's face grew blacker. Was it a warning for Matt to

100

watch every word? Matt couldn't help it, and he plunged ahead.

"Three of my men caught him at it. One of them is her brother. I guess they beat him up pretty good."

Imler sucked in a ragged breath, and that icy shade of his eyes was noticeable.

Matt thought, he doesn't believe it. He isn't going to listen.

He went ahead. "By what Lo Yen said, they gave Holden something to remember for a long time."

"Why didn't Ts'ai tell me about it?"

"She works for you," Matt said quietly. "And she is fond of Holly."

He's going to burst with rage, Matt thought, and it's all going to be directed at me. He'll order me out, or try to throw me out of the door.

"If Holden is marked as bad as Lo Yen said," he went on doggedly, "we could go see. I wouldn't mind talking to him again."

"That bastard," Imler exploded. He stood and walked with jerky steps. "I never had much use for him. He was too damned smooth. But a woman can sometimes be blind."

Matt felt limp. Imler believed him. He went all the way with Matt.

"This was hard to tell," he said. "But because of Ts'ai—" He shrugged and let that die, then started again. "I stopped him a couple of times from bothering her. But then I had to go back to work. Lo Yen stayed to protect her." He could grin now. "I guess he did a thorough job. I don't think Holden will bother her again. But I had to tell you. I thought somebody ought to keep an eye out for her."

"Don't you think I'm grateful?" Imler flared. "I saw him look at Ts'ai. She is a pretty, little thing. A man's eyes would go to her."

"Yes," Matt said.

He turned his head at the sound of the front door opening. Holly could be back, and he was lucky to have gotten it out before she returned.

101

"I'll guess I'll be going now," he said and stood.

"No, you don't," Imler said. "I want you to tell Holly about this."

"Hell no," Matt protested. "I can't do that."

"It'll carry more weight with her, if she finds out you had a part in it. If I tried to talk to her, she would just think that I was repeating some talk I heard around town. Somebody owes her more than that," he finished fiercely.

Holly came into the room alone. "Matt," she said and her eyes brightening at the sight of him.

"Tell her, Matt," Imler ordered. "Fooling around won't make it sound any better."

Her eyes darted from face to face. "What are you talking about?" she demanded.

"That damned Holden got himself in a mess," Imler said. "He tried to keep bothering Ts'ai until somebody objected to it."

Matt thought Holly's face had gone several shades whiter, and his heart ached for her.

"It's true, Holly." He forged ahead, wanting to get it all out and over. "I saw him the first time he looked at her. I warned him about it a couple of times, and he wouldn't listen. Her brother and two cousins did much more than that."

Her head still had that high, proud carriage, but her eyes were sick. "I don't believe you."

Matt made a vague, helpless gesture. "Why would I want to tell you something like this? Do you have to see it for yourself?"

Her chin was thrust forward, but he could see the tremble in it. "I don't know why you're doing this, but I don't—"

He cut her short. "—believe me." He knew she was hurt and striking back in self defense, and she looked at him with hostile eyes. He couldn't let that remain.

"You could ask Ts'ai," he said quietly.

Her eyes went wide, and red mottled her face. She took a hard breath. "I will." She raised her voice. "Ts'ai."

102

Her defiant eyes were those of an animal at bay, and he wished he didn't have to force her into this.

Ts'ai came into the room, and her eyes went around as she looked from face to face. Her face looked as though it would crumble. She knew what they had been talking about.

"I have been listening to lies, Ts'ai," Holly said. "Tell them that Gary has never bothered you."

Ts'ai tried, but her lips wouldn't form the lies. "It is true," she half-sobbed. "I did not want you to know."

She broke into tears and covered her face. Her words were muffled and broken. "He lied, saying that you were hurt and I must come to you at once. My brother and cousins beat him for it." Her crying was harder, and the rest of her words were only sound.

Matt watched Holly. Would this make her resent Ts'ai? He hoped not, but lacerated pride could be a savage master.

For an anxious moment, he thought Holly wasn't going to say anything or move. But she believed now, and its knowledge had cruelly stamped her face.

She crossed to Ts'ai and put her arms about her. "There, there," she said in a soothing voice. "Did you think I would blame you for something you couldn't help. It's all right," she said above Ts'ai's crying. "It's all right."

She led Ts'ai out of the room, and it seemed she was gone a long time.

She finally came back, and marks of crying were also on her face.

"Will you let me walk to the door with you, Matt?"

He wouldn't want a better apology. "It'll be my pleasure."

Imler wrung his hand. "We're grateful to you. Don't worry any more about Ts'ai."

"I won't," Matt said.

He stopped at the outer door and looked at Holly. "Making a mistake isn't such a bad thing. But it can be, if it wrecks us."

"It won't," she assured him. "Oh Matt! What a fool I've

103

been." She cried openly, and she made no attempt to hide the tears.

"Sho," Matt said gently. "You should see some of the ones I've made."

She tried to laugh. "Matt, will you come back?"

"You can bet on that," he said fervently.

CHAPTER FIFTEEN

Holden inspected his reflection in the mirror. His face was almost back to normal. All the swelling had vanished, and only a faint shading of the once vivid coloring remained. The long, boring wait of the ten days was about over. He could dab a little powder on the remaining color, and nobody could possibly see it.

He had holed up for those days, and only going out for the necessary meals. He had ducked everybody who knew him, and the few times he had to talk to somebody, they hadn't commented on his face. Either they were too discreet, or it wasn't as obvious as he thought it was.

Surely, nobody knew anything about his fiasco with Ts'ai, or he would have heard some comment about it. Apparently, Ts'ai hadn't talked about it. She hadn't better, he thought viciously.

Hope built in him. Was it possible that Holly didn't know? Would she believe that story about him being waylaid and beaten? If she did, it would explain his lengthy absence. His face brightened. He might salvage something out of this mess. He debated it a long moment, then nodded. It was worth the effort. He would drive to Candelaria and hope that he might run into her on the street. Until he saw her reaction he wouldn't go to the Imler house; that would be too much of a risk.

He stopped the buggy as he saw Holly coming down the street. Jubilation flooded him. Luck was running with him. After he pacified her, he would talk to Imler. Imler must be raging by now that the mill hadn't as yet reopened. The ore, from his mine, had to be piling up.

He sprang to the ground, and his old vigor was back. "Holly," he cried and hurried toward her, his hands outstretched. "If you knew how I've missed you."

He noticed that she didn't take his hands, but she wasn't frowning. That was a good sign.

"Have you?" she asked.

He couldn't analyze her tone. "It's been a bad time for both of us, Holly." He shook his head. "I guess you haven't heard what happened to me. Those footpads came at me so fast I couldn't defend myself. I was ashamed for you to see me in that condition."

"Were you?" she murmured.

Exultation leaped within him. She believed him. "I should have sent somebody to tell you, Holly. But I didn't want you worrying."

"I didn't," she said flatly. "And somebody told me."

He felt his collar growing too tight. "I didn't think anybody knew," he said haltingly. "I didn't talk to—"

She smiled at him, but there was malice in it. "Matt Norborne knew. I didn't believe him. Then Ts'ai told me everything that happened."

His face turned a mottled red and white. The names stunned him. "They're lying," he half-shouted.

"We both know better than that, don't we, Gary?" Her tone picked up force, and she lashed him with it. "How do you stand looking at yourself in a mirror? You are the most despicable man I've ever known."

His rage ran loose under the lashing. "You'd believe a couple of liars? You'll regret—"

"I already have, Gary. For ever knowing you." She turned and walked away, leaving him standing there with opened mouth. He cursed her with all the venom in his system. Being an Imler didn't make her special. A sour bile filled his mouth. He needed a drink, or several to get the taste out of his mouth.

106

Holly saw her father riding down the street and flagged him down. That was an anxious frown on Imler's face, and she shook her head.

"Nothing wrong, Dent." She blew out a breath as though she was ridding herself of a bad memory. "I just talked to Gary."

Imler scowled. "Don't tell me he had the nerve—"

She nodded. "He did. But I don't think he will ever try to again."

Imler gave her a frosty grin. Just the sight of Holden must have riled her good. He wouldn't want to face her when she was in this mood.

"Where is he? I want to talk to him."

"You don't have to," she assured him. "Let it lay, Dent."

"Not with my ore piling up like it is. I've got to find out what he's going to do."

"You're not going to deal with him after this?"

He pointed out the practical fact. "His mill is the only one around here for miles."

She didn't shake her head, but the impression was there. "Don't lose your head, Dent."

His frosty grin grew. "If you didn't, I shouldn't. Where did you see him? Is his buggy in town?"

"Two blocks down. It is," she answered both questions.

"You all right, Holly?"

"Just fine." Her smile was true.

He blew out a gusty sigh of relief. Matt Norborne could be given credit for that. It suited him fine.

He lifted the reins and moved on down the street. Holden's buggy was in front of the Roaring Gimlet Saloon. If the damned fool had any sense, he would have gotten out of town as fast as he could.

He walked into the place, and Holden was hunched over the

bar. He wondered if the man had enough time to pour down enough to put a slump like this into him? Or had Holly cut his legs from under him? Whatever it was tickled Imler. From this view he would say the man was in misery.

He touched him on the shoulder, and Holden whirled. Imler would say the man was jumpy. "Hello, Gary," he said with no emotion.

The tautness, in Holden's face, slowly decreased. Imler thought he could read Holden's mind. Holden didn't think he had talked to Holly yet.

Holden's manner loosened. "Dent, it's good to see you again."

You wouldn't think so, if you know what I know, Imler thought.

"Your mill's been down for quite a while, Gary."

Holden poured himself another drink and only remembered at the last moment to offer Imler one. Imler waved it aside.

"I've never had such a run of trouble," Holden said petulantly. "I've got some machinery that needs repairing, and I'm still hunting for the right men."

"You shouldn't have fired Sadler," Imler continued. Evidently, Sadler had spread the news of his run-in with Holden. White men wouldn't come back to work for him. He didn't know what had happened to Holden's idea of hiring Chinese.

"I'd do it again, if I had it to do over," Holden said hotly.

"I thought you were going to hire the Chinese."

"Those treacherous bastards. I found out some things about them. They can't be trusted."

Imler was sick of the man. He was steeped in self-pity and whining for sympathy. "I imagine you found out one thing. They're pretty good fighters."

Holden sucked in a breath, and his face was stark. "What do you mean by that?"

"They beat hell out of you for bothering Ts'ai."

Holden blinked as though he was suddenly dizzy. "I don't know what you're talking about."

Imler snorted. "The hell you don't." He could see one thing clearly. Holden was never going to open that mill again.

"Let me give you a piece of advice. Holden. You broke yourself. You're never going to run again. If you're smart, you'll sell out for what you can get."

Holden clutched at the bar for support. "The hell I will." His voice was high-pitched, almost a scream. "I'll be back running again, then you can take your ore some place else."

Imler's lip curled in disgust. "I was pretty sure I would have to before I came in here. Maybe I'll build one myself."

That blasted Holden with fear. He had pushed Imler too hard. If he did that, the other mine owners would go to him. He couldn't let Imler see that fear, and he sneered. "How can you do that? You haven't got the water?"

"It won't be long before I do. Matt's pushing his pipeline. I've already talked to him about it." That wasn't true, but he intended to the next time he saw Norborne.

Holden felt as though his stomach had dropped away from him. His voice was high-pitched again. "He'll never finish it. I can promise you that."

Imler spat on the floor, almost hitting Holden's boot. "You're getting to be more of a damned fool every time I see you. He'll finish it."

He turned and walked out, leaving Holden shaking with fury.

3

It was midafternoon before Holden found Sikeston. He had never had any dealings with the man, and he detested him. But even an animal like this had their use.

"Have you heard about Norborne's pipeline?" he asked without a preliminary greeting.

He grinned with evil amusement at the profanity that

spewed from Sikeston's mouth. If just the hearing of Norborne's name did this to him, what would the thinking of that pipeline crawling toward Candelaria do?

Sikeston ran down and said sullenly, "I ain't worried about it."

It's only tearing your guts out, Holden thought. "If my business was threatened with something like that, I'd put an end to it."

Sikeston looked at him with sullen eyes. It was all right for Holden to talk like this; his business didn't face this kind of a threat.

"What would you do?" he asked unwillingly.

"I'd stop it. I'd ride out there with a bunch of men and smash his camp to hell."

Sikeston wanted to make a vulger observation on that, and he managed to hold it. "Have you seen that goddamned camp? Chinks crawling all over like damned ants. How many men do you think it would take to smash it?"

"Oh, for God's sake," Holden said in disgust. "The camp's not his only vulnerable spot. He can't guard the entire line of pipe, can he? He doesn't guard the spring he gets his water from, does he?"

Sikeston looked at him thoughtfully. He couldn't let his new excitement show on his face. He too had thought of those things Holden mentioned.

"It sounds to me like you're pretty interested in that pipeline, too," he observed. "Its finishing must mean a hell of a lot to you, too."

Holden made an impatient gesture. "All right," he snapped. "I don't want to see it finished."

"I'm a poor man," Sikeston whined. "I'm barely making a living as it is. I'd need some help."

Holden stared at him in outrage. He knew what Sikeston meant about help; money. The world was filled with nothing but blood suckers.

He kept his tone level. "I'd put in five hundred dollars. If that's not enough, forget it."

He started to turn away, and Sikeston's hand clamped on his arm.

"That sounds just about right," Sikeston said eagerly. "I'll take it."

"I thought you would."

CHAPTER SIXTEEN

Two Chinese workers pulled a length of pipe out of the wagon and dropped it at the end of the former one Matt had just finished coupling onto the line. He exerted all of his strength, tightening the coupling. A man could get a lot of effort on a two-foot wrench. He kept it up until he couldn't even get a partial turn from the coupling. He had tightened all of the couplings in the line, and he wasn't worried about leakage.

"Last one on the wagon, Matt," Duncan said.

Matt didn't regret hearing that. It had been a long and hard day. Tomorrow should bring more of the same. He expected another wagonload of pipe before dark. So far, the shipments had been coming through without further trouble. He had put guards on each load, and none of them reported anything alarming. He had thought often about the ambush and the loss of the other load and had reached no conclusion about it. Would he never know who was behind it and why?

Ahead of him, Chinese were digging the ditch for the pipe to be laid in, and behind him, Chinese were filling it after the pipe had been coupled onto the rest of the line. Only the last two lengths of it would lay on top of the ground until tomorrow's work started again. He didn't know what the frost line in this country was. Back in Missouri a depth of eighteen inches was enough to be safely below it. He had dug this ditch twenty-four inches deep, and he hoped it was deep enough to withstand freezing weather. He thought of all the hours, all the shovel strokes to dig this one. Most of it had been relatively easy digging in the sand. The occasional rock took much more effort, some of them large enough to need bars to pry them out of the ground. Hell yes, it had taken a lot of work, but he could begin to see the ending of it.

"Better than two-thirds of it done, Matt," Duncan said cheerfully.

That pulled an irritable grunt from Matt. That wasn't the part of the line that concerned him. The portion, still remaining to be laid, did. He had gone over his resources a hundred times, and the closeness of the race scared him. If everything went with the best of luck, he should be in Candelaria just about the time his money ran out.

"I'll ride up and turn the valve on," Duncan said.

Matt gratefully accepted the offer. Each day the ride to the spring grew longer. And it had to be made each day. It did, if the nightly camp wanted water. That was one thing Matt could afford; ample water for any and all purposes. He stooped and started putting another valve into place at this end of the line. The spring valve would have to be turned off in the morning and this one removed. It was a small enough price to pay for the luxury of all the water a man wanted.

He lay awake a long time that night, thinking of Holly. He hadn't seen her since the day he had told her about Holden. He would see her again when the pipeline was finished. He thought she would welcome him. She hadn't put it into words, but it had been in her eyes. He grinned in the darkness. Even a slow-thinking man like himself could tell that. Beside him Duncan snored rhythmically, and Matt envied his ability to drop off to sleep so fast. He twisted and turned. Maybe he was too tired to fall asleep.

2

Sikeston's two regular helpers glanced at each other as they considered his proposal. They sat in the kitchen of his shack and drank his coffee. Odie Lawson swallowed another mouthful of coffee and grimaced. "Ryan, you sure as hell don't make the best coffee in the world."

113

He was a hulking man with a placid face. He never wanted much, and he didn't ask more than just enough to meet his needs. Sikeston had offered them fifty dollars apiece for this extra job, and Lawson didn't know whether or not it was worth it.

"What do you think, Jesse?" he asked his companion.

They made an odd pair. Jesse was a small man as shriveled as an apple that had never been picked. "I dunno," he said dubiously. "But that extra money would sure come in handy." He shook his head. "I heard that Matt Norborne is a rough one. He won't like this. The big question is, what is he going to do about it?"

Sikeston swore at the opposition. "We ain't going up to him and tell him what we're going to do. That spring is a long way from his camp. He'll be too far away to hear the dynamite go off. If it's the dynamite you're afraid of, I'll handle it. I've handled enough. I blew out a million stumps back in Ohio."

He stared moodily at them. Damned if he didn't wish he had never left Ohio. He cursed the piss and vinegar that made a young man leave the place where he had it made. Sure, farming was hard work and slow, but a man could see increasing results each year. That is, an older man could. A younger one could only see the close confines of limited vision. The hard work was still here in Nevada, and the returns were far more uncertain. Between the harsh weather and his increasing years they were grinding him thin. He was scared of Norborne's pipeline. It had kept him awake many a night. If it came through, what was he going to do?

"I dunno," Lawson said again.

Sikeston flared at them. "What are you going to do when you're out of work. Men are walking the streets right now, looking for any kind of work. I sure as hell won't need you, if Norborne finishes it."

That got to them, for they exchanged glances. Lawson heaved to his feet. "I guess we ain't got any choice, Jesse."

"Let's get it over with," Jesse growled.

"Everything's in the wagon," Sikeston said. The job wasn't

114

quite as simple as he made it sound. He wanted to do more than just dynamite the spring. But it would be smarter to wait and tell them.

Sikeston had driven the roundabout way to the spring, and he hadn't seen a soul. This would be over in the matter of minutes; the rest of the job he proposed would take much more time. But if a man was going to do a job, it should be thorough. He didn't want to just cripple Norborne. He wanted to wreck him.

He walked around the spring, making his estimation of what he had to do. A shot under the big rocks, overhanging the spring, should do it. He would put in a shot big enough to blot that spring out of existence. He scraped out a hole under the rocks with his hands, then placed his dynamite, tamping the sticks firmly into place. He fused them and looked behind him. Lawson and Jesse stood well off, watching him. His grin was a twisted thing. They were probably wondering why he had wanted them along; he was doing all the work. He would change that.

He waved them farther back before he lit the fuse. It spit into angry life, and he ran like hell. He was panting when he joined them.

"It's not going up," Lawson said.

Lawson had a thick head, and Sikeston swore at him. It took a little time for fire to run along a fuse. "Goddamnit! Give it—"

The blast blotted out the rest of his words, momentarily lighting up the night with a display of light that even awed him. He had never shot off dynamite at night. The earth heaved upward, shooting up a geyser of water, rock, and sand. Even this far away a shard of rock whizzed by his head, and he ducked. The light disappeared, and he heard the thud of rock falling back to earth. Dynamite always had that acrid smell, and it carried to Sikeston.

The shattering blast, the dazzling light and the geyser of debris tickled Lawson. "She went up good, didn't she?"

115

Jesse was a more practical man. "That finishes it, doesn't it?"

"Not quite," Sikeston corrected him. He walked to the spot where the spring had been, and they followed him. He was filled with wicked satisfaction as he looked at it. He had no idea of how many tons of rock and sand had covered the spring, but he would bet it was several feet. A pungent, penetrating smell hung over everything. The spring was no longer running. Perhaps some of the sand was moist, for it looked blacker than the surrounding sand. Sure, the water might work its way back to the surface, but it could also be entirely lost.

Jesse asked another of his practical questions. "Can't he dig it out?"

"If he can find it. But that'll take him time and money. If he does, I'll blow it up again. That ain't all I'm going to dump on him."

Lawson didn't like the sound of that at all. "If we keep fooling around with him, he's liable to shoot us. What are you planning next?"

"Just digging up that spring won't be all he's up against. We'll dig up a long length of his line, pile up the pipe, and find out what dynamite does with it."

He grinned fiendishly at their hollow groans. Now they knew now why he had brought them along.

3

Matt came groggily awake as Duncan shook his shoulder. He sat up and stared toward the east. A faint line of the first, false light of dawn was on the horizon. "What the hell," he said in half anger. Duncan had awakened him a good hour before the usual time.

"Matt, I woke up and couldn't get back to sleep." That was apology in his tone. "You know how a man can think of the damnedest things. I lay there and thought of water, cold water."

116

"Oh God," Matt said in disgust. "All you had to do was to walk over and turn on the valve."

"I did," Duncan said quietly. "Maybe a few drops came out but not enough to cover the bottom of a tin cup.

That drove the last of the sleep fog from Matt's eyes. "You're sure."

Duncan accepted the judging of his sanity calmly enough. "I'm sure."

Matt threw the blanket from him and tugged on his boots. Maybe the valve was stuck, maybe Duncan hadn't turned it right. He could make a dozen more such explanations and knew all of them were worthless. Something had happened.

He walked over to the valve and turned it. It worked easily enough. No corrosion was binding it. He ran his fingers around the lip of the pipe. He felt moisture but no water.

"What do you think it is, Matt?"

Matt shook his head. "Some blockage of some kind, Riley. Maybe silt got in and fouled up the upper valve."

"I'll ride out and see, Matt."

"Both of us, Riley." Matt didn't know what the trouble was, but it could take both of them to clear it up.

He saddled, and Duncan was doing the same. Duncan started to swing up, and Matt said, "Better bring your rifle along."

"You expecting that kind of trouble?"

"I don't know what I'm expecting. But just take it along with you."

They rode along the pipeline, and even in the darkness, the mound of the filled-in ditch was discernible. It would take a lot of weather to settle it. Matt wondered if he was going to have trouble with the valves after he finished the line into Candelaria.

He kept his horse moving at a fast clip, and the miles fell behind them. The light was beginning to strengthen in the eastern sky. He would say they were less than two miles from the spring.

The blast of an explosion shattered the still of the dawn,

117

and Matt jerked his horse to a stop. The darkness was momentarily lifted up by a great flash of light.

"What the hell was that?" Duncan gasped.

Matt didn't know, but a fear froze his guts. It sounded like some kind of explosion. It had affected the horses too, for they danced nervously. He had heard blasts like that before, and it had to come from a powder or dynamite explosion. It came from right up ahead, and the mound of the ditch ran straight toward it.

Matt jerked his rifle from its scabbard. "We'd better go see." He sunk his heels into the horse's flanks. He didn't worry about the horse stepping into a hole and falling. He had a far greater worry now.

They hadn't gone a quarter of a mile when Duncan yelled, "Something up ahead."

Matt had seen it, three moving, darting blobs against the weak light. Three figures were running toward a bigger shadow, and Matt would guess that could be a wagon. He reined the horse to a stop. Shooting from the back of a running horse at a running target made for poor results. He heard Duncan do the same. He didn't know who those men were, or what they had to do with the explosion, but they had a hand in it some way.

"Hold it," he yelled. They had to hear him, but they kept running. He had the rifle butt snugged against his shoulder. He had something that would stop them. He centered on one of the figures and squeezed the trigger. The running figure stopped suddenly as though it had run into a stone wall. It threw its arms high, whirled and slumped to the ground.

Duncan missed his first shot, for Matt heard him swear. Duncan fired again, and a second figure bent lower and lower, until the next reaching stride crumbled under him, and he went down.

The third running man made the wagon and darted around it. Matt thought he was going to put up some kind of a defense from it, then the figure appeared, clambering up onto

118

the seat. He lashed the horses, then hunched low over the reins.

Matt's rifle sight followed him. "I'll take him," he said to Duncan. The crack of the rifle was thin and volumeless compared to a big explosion.

For a moment, he thought he had missed, then the figure reared high in the box, grabbing for invisible handfuls to support him. He hung there a long moment as the horses pounded on, then pitched sideways out of the wagon.

"That's all of them," Duncan said.

Duncan was right, but it didn't ease the grip of the terrible fear. What had they done?

The wagon was still careening away, and Matt said, "Catch it up, Riley, while I check on these three."

Duncan set out on a hard gallop after the wagon. Matt rode to the first figure on the ground. The man was groaning. Matt turned him over with the toe of his boot, and it was Lawson. It didn't surprise him. This one named the other two for him.

"My shoulder," Lawson groaned. "It's all busted to hell. Oh God, do something for me."

Matt put the rifle muzzle between Lawson's eyes. "I ought to blow your goddamned brains out. You try to lie to me, and I will."

Lawson's face was stamped with mortal terror. "I didn't want to come along. Sikeston made me. I told him we'd run into big trouble."

"You've run into it," Matt said grimly. "What did he do?"

Words poured out of Lawson in a rush. "He blew up your spring. But that didn't satisfy him. We had to dig up your line, pile it up, and blow it up, too."

Matt's rage shook him, and it was all he could do to keep from pressing the trigger. "How much did you dig up?"

"A long way," Lawson said vaguely.

Matt fought off the sickness of the rage, and a dull resignation filtered in. Maybe he was through building the line. It depended upon how much damage had been done.

119

He raised the rifle muzzle, and Lawson begged, "You can't just let me lay here."

"Don't tempt me," Matt growled. He looked in the direction Duncan had taken. Duncan had caught the wagon. He had tied his horse on behind it, and he was swinging the wagon in a wide circle to bring it back.

Matt took a step, and Lawson screamed, "You can't do this. You wouldn't walk away and leave me."

Matt looked back at him. "You keep pushing your luck."

He walked to the next body, and this one wouldn't talk to anybody. He stared dispassionately at Jesse, then walked to the third one.

Sikeston lay face down, and Matt didn't turn him over. His aim had been good. He had hit Sikeston between the shoulder blades.

"You worthless bastard," he said wearily. All the heat of his rage had gone out of him, leaving him drained.

He could see lengths of pipe up ahead, and he walked to them. They were scattered all over the desert as though in sudden rage, a giant hand had thrown a handful of matches away. Sikeston must have used a lot of dynamite. Some of the lengths were split, and others were bent and twisted. Matt didn't see any one of them that could be reused. Lawson was right when he said they had dug up a long way.

He stood at the crater, blasted out by the dynamite, and had more shipments of pipe coming in, but this finished him. his eyes were dull with the sickness this caused him. He He had only enough pipe to finish the line; not enough to repair this vandalism.

He heard the rumble of wheels and turned and walked over to where Duncan was just pulling up. Duncan's eyes swept over the three figures on the ground. "Who are they, Matt?"

"Maybe the ones we should have suspected," Matt said in a tired vice. "Sikeston. Lawson and Jesse were with him." He forestalled another question. "Sikeston and Jesse are dead. Lawson's got a hole in his shoulder. He'll live." He looked over at Lawson. "Though he probably needs some attention right now."

The need didn't stir Duncan any more than it had him. Duncan cursed them with every foul word he could find. When he ran down, he asked, "They set that explosion?"

Matt nodded.

"Did it do a lot of damage?"

Matt barely caught his flare of temper. Duncan had eyes, didn't he. He could see the ruined pipe.

He softened his tone. Duncan hadn't been able to inspect it up close. He made a weary gesture. "All they needed to do, Riley. It finishes us."

"Aw, Matt. Maybe you're jumping too quick." A look at Matt's face told him that hope was false. His shoulders slumped, and his head drooped. He looked at the reins in his hands as though he had never seen such things before. "Hell, Matt, we can lay more pipe."

Duncan was only trying to be cheerful, but it honed Matt's temper. "Where are we going to get the money to buy it. With all the good luck in the world on our side, we could have barely made it. This isn't the worse damage they did. They blew up the spring."

Duncan's mouth was shocked open, and he couldn't form a word with it. He finally managed to say, "What do we do now?"

Matt didn't know, and right now, he couldn't bear to think about it. "We'll have to get them," he jerked his head toward the two bodies, "and Lawson into town. I'll help you load them."

They picked up Sikeston and Jessie and put them into the bed of the wagon. Duncan pointed at the partial case of dynamite and the shovels and wrenches. "He came supplied well enough, didn't he?"

"Well enough," Matt said flatly.

He tore off the good sleeve of Lawson's shirt and by using his and Lawson's handkerchief, made a crude bandage and tied it into place.

121

"I didn't want to do it," Lawson kept saying. "I tried to tell him—"

"Shut up," Matt said fiercely. "Just keep your damned mouth shut. Aren't you satisfied at being lucky enough to still be alive?"

Lawson's terrified eyes went to his face, and he shut his mouth.

Matt and Duncan picked him up, and they handled him more gently than they had the other two.

"Take them in, Riley," Matt said. "You might as well break camp. Tell Lo Yen and the others the work's over."

"There's a shipment of pipe coming in," Duncan cried.

"I'll wait for it," Matt said in a dead voice. "Maybe we can salvage a little money out of it." And the other things, he thought; the tools, the wagons, and the horses.

"Where are you going now?" Duncan called as Matt walked toward his horse.

Matt looked back. "I'm going out to see how bad the spring is."

Duncan wanted to say more; it was in his face. Matt was grateful that he didn't.

He rode out to the spring, and the enormity of the damage increased the sickness. Where a spring had flowed was now only a jumble of rock. He sat there a long time, looking at the ruin. That might be a spot of moisture, but it wasn't increasing, and the rising sun would wipe it out.

He felt numb all over. Of course, it might be dug out, if he had the men to hire. That took money. He couldn't even find enough resentment left to swear at Sikeston. He guessed this was the way a man's dream ended—in a jumble of piled-up rock.

He slowly wheeled his horse. He didn't want to think of Holly Imler, or any of the rest of it. He was lonely enough as it was.

CHAPTER SEVENTEEN

Lo Yen was the last of the Chinese to be paid off, and his face was heavy with distress. Matt was wrong when he thought the Chinese were an inscrutable race. Lo Yen hurt for him and bad.

Lo Yen shook his head at the money Matt offered him. "Keep it. It may help—"

Matt grinned painfully. "This wouldn't be anywhere enough, Lo Yen. But thanks anyway."

He pressed the money into Lo Yen's hand. Lo Yen looked at it before he dropped it into his pocket. "If you find a way, I'd like to work for you. All the men would."

"Sure," Matt said gruffly. "You'll be the first I let know." He slapped Lo Yen's shoulder before he left him. He hoped the gesture would say more to Lo Yen than any of the feeble words he had been able to say.

If he could find a way, Lo Yen had said. My God! He had searched every avenue he could think of. He had gone down each one until he found it was blocked. He had had a couple of offers to back him until he found out what it would cost him. One of them wanted fifty percent of the line, the other only a mere seventy-five percentage. Those two men had shrewdly guessed at the bind he was in. That uncompleted pipeline still lay out there. All they had to do was to wait around until Matt abandoned it. He groaned in pure misery. If they only knew how close he was to that now.

He had gotten an offer for the tools, the wagons and horses, and the smallness of it was an open insult. They knew he was helpless. The goddamned vultures were gathering to strip his carcass.

Duncan came down the street, and one look at his face

told Matt Duncan hadn't had any more success in selling the equipment.

"Nothing, Matt," he said. "They act like I'm some kind of an idiot. You should hear what they offered me."

"I know," Matt said wearily. He should. He had just gone through the same thing.

They had been in town a little less than a week, and so far it had been fruitless. Matt didn't know where else to turn. Sure, he had thought of Dent Imler. But he couldn't go to him because Holly was involved. That would be a form of begging, and Matt couldn't face that.

"Come on down with me to Lily's, Matt. A few drinks, a few laughs."

And a woman, Matt thought. That might lift Duncan temporarily out of his depression. It wouldn't do a thing for Matt.

He managed a smile, and it didn't extend from his lips. "You go ahead, Riley. You got any money?"

"Enough, Matt. Did you need some?"

Matt shook his head. They both grieved over the same bier, but their sorrowing needed different solace.

He jingled the coins in his pocket as he watched Duncan until he was out of sight. He was reaching the stage where they were almost as abundant as the bills he had.

"Why not?" he asked himself. He had gone through enough to buy him a forgetfulness. He admitted its weakness, but sometimes a man had to run away from his thoughts.

He walked into the Roaring Gimlet and pulled a few crumpled bills from his pocket. "Leave the bottle, Sam."

He didn't miss the weighing in Sam's eyes and knew what he thought. Something was prodding Matt hard. It wasn't often that he went on a tear.

He splashed the whole glass into his mouth with one drink, and had to wait a moment to clear his eyes and throat. The thoughts were still with him. He would have to do better to lower the level of the bottle, or those thoughts wouldn't be blotted out.

124

After a few drinks, he found that the depression lifted. He had been in tight spots before and had always been able to wriggle free. Why was this one any different? He was aware of what made the crutch that was bolstering him, but damnit. It was working, wasn't it?"

He whirled at the touch on his shoulder, and his expression was belligerent. The news of his crash had to be all over town by now, and he didn't want any conversation about it with anybody. A lot of men had professed how sorry they were, but Matt hadn't missed the glint of malice in their eyes. That was typical of so much of the human race. They liked to see a man pulled down.

"Dent wants to see you," Tipton said.

Matt squinted at him. This was the man who had brought the first summons; he was the one who had started all of his troubles. That wasn't quite true, but things had started turning bad for him right after that. He had met Holly at the Imler house, and he wished he hadn't. His hands had been empty then too, but he had a dream to go with them. Now he just had the empty hands.

"You tell Dent if he wants to see me to come down here."

Shock turned Tipton's face blank, and he fumbled for words. "I don't know how he'll take that. Usually—"

He didn't finish, and Matt wanted to hoot at him. He knew what Tipton left unsaid. Usually, a man didn't refuse Dent Imler anything.

"Tell him what I said." He turned back and poured himself another drink. The level in the bottle was lowering nicely.

He had no idea of how much time had passed when another hand touched him. This was more authoritative; it clamped on his shoulder. Was that damned Tipton back with another summons? If so, the man was getting brash.

He turned slowly, and Imler grinned at him. "You put Tipton in a state of shock," he said cheerfully.

"To hell with him." Matt articulated each word with care. He wanted no doubt left in Imler's head as to how he felt.

125

If there was the smallest contact with any of the Imlers left, he wanted to smash it good.

He was amazed. That seemed to increase Imler's grin, and he turned it over fuzzily in his mind.

While he was pondering on that, Imler said, "You're feeling sorry for yourself, Matt." He looked at the bottle's level. "That won't drown it. Not for long anyway."

It made Matt angry, and he could feel its heat stealing into his face. "You don't know what happened." He broke that off. That sounded as though he was begging, and he didn't want that. "My business, Dent."

"It sure is," Imler agreed amiably. "Won't you even talk to me?"

Matt couldn't refuse him that, and he said unwillingly, "Pour yourself a drink."

"An offer I never turn down," Imler said.

It wasn't good whiskey, and both of them knew it, but Imler kept his face smooth.

"I guess you've heard about it." That ungracious note was back in Matt's tone.

"Could I help it? It's all over town."

Matt reached for the bottle. "I guess it is." Damn, but that hurt. Holly would know about it, too. He raised the glass and closed one eye at it as though he was making a keen appraisal.

"Sikeston did a thorough job," he muttered. He flushed with the realization that sounded like another bid for sympathy.

Imler nodded. "How much did it set you back?"

Matt's eyes sparked. Didn't Imler understand plain English? "I said he did a thorough job. I can't finish it."

Imler had something he wanted to say, but he looked around at the other men in the room and held it.

"Matt, I haven't had breakfast yet. Will you join me?"

The bottle wasn't empty yet. "I'm not hungry," Matt growled.

"You could join me for a cup of coffee, couldn't you?"

Matt wanted to refuse and held it. It wasn't Imler's fault that he was in this bind.

"All right," he conceded and moved away from the bar.

"You're leaving your bottle," Imler reminded him.

"Maybe I've had enough." Things were getting fuzzy, and his feet didn't track the way Matt ordered them.

He stumbled, crossing the street to Burrill's Cafe, and Imler caught his arm.

That fused Matt's temper, and he flared. "I didn't ask for any help."

"All of us have to one time or another, Matt," Imler said quietly.

He sat across the table from Matt and ordered coffee for both of them. "It was bad, huh, Matt?"

Matt drank the cup before he answered. "Bad enough. I had enough money to finish it. It won't stretch to repair the damage."

"I talked to Holden the other day, Matt."

Matt felt a resentment at the abrupt change of subject. That sympathy wasn't as genuine as he supposed.

"I doubt he's going to reopen his mill. He can't get the help he needs."

That makes two of us in a similiar spot, Matt thought. Holden can't get help, and I can't get money. "I'm not bleeding too much for him," he growled and signaled Burrill to bring another cup of coffee.

Imler shook his head in mock sorrow. "You're not putting things together well this morning, are you? Can't you understand what I'm telling you?"

Matt scowled at him. He had heard every word Imler said, and none of it was his concern.

Imler laughed at his expression. "With Holden's mill closed that leaves me with the prospect of a long shipping to some other mill. Or building one of my own."

Matt wasn't interested. Every man had a problem of his own.

127

"You are hardheaded this morning," Imler said with amusement. "I'd build one in a minute, if I had ample water." Matt stared at him, trying to sort this out. What was Imler trying to tell him?

"So I looked around to find out where I could get the water. You know where I found the answer? From the pipeline Matt Norborne's building."

"Are you saying—" He thought that was a false lead and backed up from it. "Are you offering me money?" That was pretty blunt, but he could think of no better way to put it.

"I'll back you for all you need."

There it was in plain words. But it didn't wipe out all of the suspicions. The past few days had taught him that every man pounded on his own anvil.

"What percentage do you want?"

Imler shook his head in exasperation. "You think I'm trying to walk on you while you're down? I'm not asking for any percentage. I'm offering you a loan until you get on your feet. You finish your line, and I get my water. That's all."

He sat back, smiling as Matt tried to plow through all of this.

Matt finally convinced himself that he had heard everything correctly. "Done," he said hoarsely and thrust out his hand. A remnant of the old suspicions remained. "Did Holly put you up to this?"

Imler's grip closed on Matt's hand. "What if she had? Would your damned pride keep you from accepting it? But she didn't. She was worried about you. But after I talked to Holden I knew what I had to do. I waited until I saw how things turned out for you. A man likes to finish what he started on his own. But if you don't want—" He let a shrug finish for him.

"I do," Matt said and wrung Imler's hand again.

"Do you suppose you'd come up to the house now? We've got a few details to settle."

128

"I'm with you," Matt said happily. A new thought struck him. He didn't want Holly seeing him looking like this. "I'll be there in an hour or so."

At the small frown on Imler's face he explained, "I'd like to get a haircut, shave, and a bath. And maybe some new clothes." That would take money. Who was worried about money now?

Imler chuckled. "I'd say with that kind of a motivation a man can't be far wrong. I'll be waiting for you."

Matt beat him out of the door. He had a lot to do, and the time he had given Imler wouldn't be too long.

He felt resplendent and assured in his new clothes. But that was only outward, for the shakiness was within him. Imler had given him his dream back, and he wanted to ask Holly if she would share it with him.

She answered his knock on the door, and her eyes were radiant. Matt saw Imler behind her, and Imler suddenly ducked out of sight. Imler was a discerning man. The more Matt saw of him, the more he approved of him.

"Holly," he said, and the rest of the words stuck in his throat.

"Oh, Matt," she breathed. "Dent told me. Isn't it fine?"

How had she gotten this close to him? He was certain he hadn't moved to her, and to the best of his knowledge, she hadn't either.

Her head was tilted up to him, and the invitation was in her shining eyes and her parted lips.

He was going too fast, he warned himself. But he couldn't help himself. He bent forward and kissed her. Her lips were warm and trembling, but they gave him the same promise he gave her.

She pulled away from him, and the heightened color was rosy in her face.

Too fast, he thought mournfully. "Didn't I tell you so?"

But she hadn't pulled away from his arms. She came back

to him and buried her face in his chest. "Matt, I'm shameless. We've known each other such a short time."

"Me, too," he confessed. His laughter was full and true. "Should we waste any more time?"

Her lips answered that to his full satisfaction. She pulled away again and said, "We're keeping Dent waiting."

"Do you care?"

"Not if you don't," she answered. She lifted her mouth again.

He was filled with a tremulous awe. How could everything a man ever dreamed of happen all at once?

CHAPTER EIGHTEEN

Cleaver had always had sneaky eyes, and they had that sly look in them as he looked across the card table to Holden.

"Gary, how come you never go over to Candelaria any more?" He dealt another round of cards. "You used to be over there all the time. What happened?"

Holden snatched up the cards, the viciousness in him showing by his manner. The faces around the table were blank, but he thought there were snickers behind them.

"Did we come here to play cards or talk?" he snarled.

"Why, Gary, you know I'm always glad to see you come in," Cleaver said mockingly. "My pockets are glad to see you, too."

The furtive grins were appearing now, and it put a wildness in Holden's eyes. He had been bucking Cleaver's game heavily for the two past weeks, and it was costing him. He shuddered every time he thought of the money it had cost him. Could luck be running that bad consistently against him. Several times, he had thought that Cleaver must be cheating, but he was wise enough not to put that accusation into words. Cleaver was one tough man, and that reputation was well-founded. If Holden ever dared open his mouth with something like that, Cleaver would call him out and shoot him dead.

"Deal the cards," he said in a cracked voice.

Cleaver dealt another round and said, "Open."

Holden stared at his hand with rage-infested eyes. This was another handful of garbage, like so many before had been. "I can't," he muttered as it came around to him.

"Well, I can," Cleaver said, tossing ten dollars into the pot. "It'll cost you that much, if you stay."

Holden tossed in his hand with a muttered oath.

"Your luck seems to be running bad all the way, Gary," Cleaver said in that same mocking vein. "From the talk I gather, you seem to have lost your woman. I heard that Norborne has moved in on you."

Holden glared at him. Cleaver was a squat, broad man with the long, supple fingers of the born gambler. He ran this saloon, but Holden doubted that if he was concerned with its profit or loss. This game was all he needed to keep him going.

"To hell with Norborne," Holden said thickly.

All the snickers were open now. Even Cleaver had trouble keeping the grin off of his face.

"No takers?" he asked. He shrugged, displayed a pair of queens, and raked in the pot. "A small one, but if a man wins enough of them, it'll keep the wolf away from his door."

He looked at Holden with a sardonic speculation. "What's keeping the wolf away from your door now, Gary? With your mill shut down it must be cutting into you."

It was, Holden admitted, but he would never admit it to them. He had spent many a sleepless hour twisting and turning over it.

"You should have sold out while you had the chance," Cleaver murmured. "I'll bet it would have brought a good price. It sure won't bring much, if Imler builds one."

Holden's collar felt tight, and he wanted to loosen it. But that would be an open admission that Cleaver's taunting was getting through to him.

"He won't," he said and tried to put a confidence into his voice. "Where's he going to get his water."

Cleaver's eyebrows quirked. "Haven't you heard? People are saying that Imler's backing Norborne. I heard only yesterday morning that Norborne's got the spring dug out and running. All he's waiting for now is for more pipe to arrive."

Holden slammed his fist against the table, shoved his chair behind him, and stood. "I'm telling you one thing," he said

132

wildly. "Imler won't build that mill, and Norborne won't finish that pipeline."

He caught the questioning looks they threw at each other and managed to catch himself.

"Tell us how you're going to stop them," Cleaver said with bright, false interest.

"You wait and see," Holden said thickly and turned and plunged for the door.

"Sounds like he's gone out of his head," one of the players observed.

"He might be at that," Cleaver said. "When everything was going good for him, he wouldn't think of coming into a place like this." He hawked and spat on the floor beside him. "Now that he hasn't any place else to go, he favors us with his presence."

"You prodded him pretty good, Cleaver," one of the players said.

"I did, didn't I?" Self-satisfaction was evident in Cleaver's voice. "His damned airs always made me sick." He hooted with laughter. "Did you hear what he said. He's going to stop Imler and Norborne. I'd say that's a big mouthful to chew off."

Laughter ran all around the table. "You've probably lost a player, Cleaver."

Cleaver shrugged. "Who's mourning? Deal the cards."

Holden cursed Cleaver and the others. If they were talking about him like that in his own town, he could imagine what Candelaria was saying. Just the thought of it ran a red-hot barb deep into his flesh. There might have been some guessing in Cleaver's talk, but it was damned accurate guessing.

"I'll show every damned one of them." His voice was louder than usual, and he knew the source of that, too. The ghostly silence of the mill haunted him.

He was scared of looking at the future, and every passing day brought him that much closer when he had to. He had a list of names that equally earned his hating. It included

133

Norborne and Imler, Ts'ai and her brother. Yes, he had enough room left in that hating to include Holly. She had turned away from him just when he had most needed her.

He looked at his hands. They were so tightly fisted that the knuckles stood out in stark relief. "I'd like to hurt all of them," he said aloud. "I'd like to smash them."

He could say it a million times, but the words were hollow unless he could do something about them. He would like to include Candelaria in that smashing. The town had never brought him anything but trouble and misery. How he would like to see that town lying in ruins. He stopped short. An idea was forming in his head. He couldn't clearly see all of it, but it was building. He couldn't destroy Candelaria by himself, but he could solicit others to do it for him. His eyes glistened as the details came into view. Hungry bellies would listen to somebody who pointed out a way to get out of their misery. What would be the easiest and quickest way to make men follow him? A race riot! He sucked in his breath at the brilliancy of his thinking. There it was in two simple words. The different races hated each other enough without anybody needing to pour kerosene on the fire. All he had to do was to point out to the whites that the Chinese were responsible for the unemployment. Men would listen to that. Burn the damned yellow-skins' houses and drive them out of town. Then the jobs that were left would rightfully belong to the whites.

He could see the scene in his mind's eyes, and his gloating grew. It didn't take much to enflame a mob. A few well-chosen words, pointing out who was responsible for their plight, and that mob would begin to roar. Once that poisoned seed was planted in their heads, violent action had to follow. When the first torch was applied, the mob would be unleashed, and nothing could stop it, until the town was going up in flames. Heads would be broken, bodies battered, and men would die. The wildness would run until the blood lust was satiated.

"Yes," he shouted at the top of his voice. That would pay

134

back all that was owed him. If a major part of the town burned, why couldn't Imler's house be part of it? It was all in place now, and his eyes glistened. All it would take was to find the right men. He thought of two men who exactly fit the role. Even with them it would take a careful tilling of the soil, but if it was handled right, how the seed would grow. He grabbed his hat and jammed it on his head.

He looked in a half-dozen saloons before he found the Barrett brothers. They were known to be ne'er-do-wells, unable to hold a job for long. He thought of Steiger. He had used men of this caliber before.

He noticed before he went into the last saloon that the streets of Candelaria teemed with traffic, much more than usual. Men surged up and down the streets with an apparent restlessness. These men had nothing to do except walk the streets, and the bitterness of having no job drove them. The tinder was ready; all it needed was the application of the right spark.

The Barrett brothers were seated at a rear table in the saloon. Their faces were heavy with brooding, and a partially empty mug of beer was before each of them. Holden knew why they drank beer. They couldn't afford anything else.

"Hello, men," he said, stopping at their table.

He wasn't surprised at their animosity. He was in that hated class; he was an employer.

Neither of them returned his greeting, nor invited him to sit down. They were cast in the same mold, dirty, disheveled men with scraggly hair and unshaven beards.

He pulled out a chair and asked, "Mind if I join you?"

"What for?" Hige Barrett growled. He was the older and bigger of the two. Whatever he did, Coe Barrett followed him.

"I thought I'd buy a bottle." Holden shrugged. "If you don't—" He turned as though to start away.

"Wait a minute," Coe Barrett yelped. He had a mouthful of bad teeth. "Sure, we'd be glad to have you. Wouldn't we, Hige?"

Hige grumbled something, then said ungraciously, "Sit down."

"Wait until I bring a bottle back." Holden walked to the bar, debating upon the brand. Not the most expensive; the Barretts weren't used to it.

He came back with three glasses and the bottle. "This ought to make a man forget his troubles."

They had an animal's wariness, and they waited for him to make the next move.

Holden poured the three glasses full, pushed two of them toward the Barretts, and lifted his own. "Here's to happy days."

"In this goddamned town?" Hige Barrett snarled. But he reached for his glass.

He downed it in a gulp and wiped the back of his hand across his mouth. "Good whiskey." His tone wasn't as hostile.

This was rotten whiskey, and Holden had to struggle to keep it from showing on his face. He pushed the bottle toward Hige. "Go ahead. I bought it for us."

Hige's suspicion wasn't entirely erased, but he filled his glass. "Why?" he demanded.

Holden burned inwardly. These damned animals were as wily as the four-legged kind. "Just to talk to somebody who's in the same fix I am."

"You?" Coe said incredulously. Holden was in a class these two could never reach. He was a wealthy man, he was a property owner.

Holden thought he had correctly read them. "You think being a mill owner makes it easier for me? My God, if you knew the worries I have."

Their shaking heads said how much they disagreed with him. When a man reached Holden's level, there wasn't anything left to worry about.

"Look at how long I've been shut down," Holden said. "Nothing coming in and everything going out."

"I heard that's your fault," Hige growled.

Holden looked astounded. "Lies, I suppose spread by

136

Sadler. He shut me down. Don't tell me you two listen to him, too."

"Not us," Coe cried. "Him and his goddamned union. What's it done for us?"

Holden had his opening. "Don't you see? We're just alike. I'd hire you two in a minute, but two men can't run a mill. But we can't blame all this unemployment on Sadler alone."

Hige frowned as he poured another glass. "Who do we blame then?"

"Men like Norborne and Imler. They went out and hired the Chinese. It's getting so a white man won't work beside them. The yellow monkeys will work for half the wage a white man deserves. They're animals and like animals, they can live cheaper."

Hige and Coe looked at each other and nodded in solemn agreement.

"Hey, Hige," Coe said in delight. "He talks our language."

"That's why my mill is shut down," Holden said. "I could have hired Chinks and maybe even have taught them to run it. I might have been able to run it cheaper, but I wouldn't let them on my place."

He had them now, for the last of the suspicion was gone from their eyes. Those two made a fast inroad on a bottle. It didn't matter. When this one was gone, Holden would buy another.

He poured his second drink and sipped it slowly, steeling himself for the onslaught the raw and potent stuff would make on his throat and stomach. "Do you know what I told Imler and all the others like his kind? I told him he wouldn't run any of his ore through my mill as long as he had a single Chink on his payroll."

Hige was beginning to slur an occasional word, but his capacity for whiskey hadn't seemed to lessen. "By God, we need more big men like you around. No white man would walk around with an empty belly, then."

"I wish I could do something about it," Holden said regretfully. "But I can't all by myself." His face was grave and concerned, but wicked laughter flooded him. He had their attention; every word he said from now on would be important to them.

"What would you do?" Coe asked.

"If I had the backing, I'd run every Chink out of town. I'd make it so hot for them that from now every damned one of them would be scared to show his face around here."

Hige hit the table with his fist, and the glasses danced. Only Coe's quick grab saved the bottle from overturning. "Don't get that worked up," he grumbled.

Hige raised his voice. "That's the kind of talk I like to hear. Run every damned one of them out of town." He poured another drink into that bottomless pit, and a few drops ran down his chin. His eyes had a dull shine, and they kept drifting from Holden's face. "Just how would you go about it?"

Holden raised his hands and let them fall. "I told you I'm helpless. There's too few men who think like you do."

"How would you start?" Hige insisted.

"I'd talk to everybody I could until I found enough men who had enough guts to do something. When I had them, I'd move. I'd beat hell out of every Chinaman I saw, I'd burn down his house. One night of that would be enough to send them fleeing like mice."

Hige glanced at his brother, and there was admiration in his eyes. "He's got a head on him, ain't he?" He scowled as Coe drained the last of the bottle. "Damnit! If you ain't turning into a hog."

Holden listened with disgust to their bickering. Animals, he thought again. They can't hold an idea in their head for two minutes.

"I'll go get another one," he said.

Hige considered it, then shook his head. "I guess we got enough for tonight."

"Yes, but how about the morning? A man needs a drink to face the day on."

"Hige, you gonna argue with the man?" Coe asked.

"I guess not," Hige said, and his broken teeth showed. "It looks like to me that he's got all the answers to every problem."

Holden kept his face wooden. The seed was planted in fertile soil. He might have to do a little more cultivating to make it flourish. But had he expected it to be easy?

He bought the bottle, handed it to Hige, and walked out with them. "Which way are you going?" he asked. "Good," he said as Hige vaguely gestured. "I'm going that way. I'll walk with you."

The first bottle was working on them hard. Hige lurched as he walked, and Coe kept trying to sing until Hige yelled at him to shut up.

A figure in dark clothing came around the corner ahead and walked toward them. Now was as good a time as any to see how well he had planted.

He pointed to the Chinese. "Here comes one of the little, grinning foreigners now. What'll you bet? He'll bow and scrape and step aside to let us pass. But that doesn't cost him anything. While he's showing all his manners he's taking the bread out of our mouths.

"You think so?" Hige howled. He shoved the bottle into Coe's hands. "I'll show you."

The Chinese was close enough for Holden to make out his features. Broad daylight wouldn't have made any difference. He couldn't tell one from the other. But he was right about that bowing and scraping. His head bobbed repeatedly, and he siddled to the outside, hoping to pass them there.

"You goddamned heathen," Hige yelled. "You steal into this country, then try to steal everything you can from a good American. I'll show you how much you can get by with it."

Alarm was beginning to form on the man's face. Maybe he didn't understand what Hige said, but his attitude was plain enough. Hige hit him squarely in the face, knocking him down and out into the street.

Holden watched it with cold dispassion. This was only the beginning.

He didn't expect to see the Chinese get up, but the man was more durable than Holden thought. He lit and rolled, then came up to his hands and knees, shaking his head to clear it.

Coe roared with obscene laughter. "You couldn't even put that little-bitty man out, Hige. Don't go out there. He might hit you back."

"I'll show you," Hige yelled in wild rage. "I'll kick his damned head off."

He ran out into the street, and the Chinese was still on his hand and knees. He saw Hige coming and scurried away on his hands and knees. Hige caught up with him three times, and each time, he stopped and aimed a kick at him. He had no success with any of the kicks, and while he was recovering his balance, the Chinese put new distance between them.

Hige came back after his last miss, and he was raging. "How can you fight one of the little yellow devils? They won't stand still."

His eyes narrowed as he stared at Holden. "I'm beginning to think the way you do. I'd like to talk to you again tomorrow night."

"My pleasure," Holden said. The wicked laughter rechoed within him. He had planted well in a fertile soil.

CHAPTER NINETEEN

Holly met Matt at the door, and the fact that Imler stood behind her, didn't deter Matt. Imler wasn't a stupid man. He knew what was between them, and he had made no prior objections.

Matt hugged her, picked her up, and whirled around.

"Holly, it looks like you're getting a wild man," Imler said acidly.

Holly's face was rosy when Matt put her back on her feet. "Do you hear me complaining?" she asked her father and lifted her lips to Matt.

"Don't pay any attention to me," Imler said and stalked toward the parlor. "I'm just her father," he said over his shoulder. "I shouldn't know what's going on."

Holly laughed as she exchanged glances with Matt. "Do you think we should tell him?"

Matt's face was grave, but his eyes were shining. "You're only his daughter. I don't think he'd be interested. But maybe we should tell him. You know how Dent is. He doesn't like to be left out of things." He took her hand, and they followed Imler.

At first, Matt thought Imler was sulking, then he saw the humor crinkles radiating from his eyes.

Imler held up his hand as Matt started to speak. "Don't tell me anything. I'm the last one to know what's going on."

Holly took a deep breath. "Dent, Matt and I had a long talk when he was here last night."

"What's so different about last night? He's here every night."

Matt was too happy a man for anybody to dig him. "Why shouldn't I be here, Dent? The end of the pipeline is only a

141

couple of miles out of town. I'd ride a whole lot farther than that to see her."

Imler peered from one to the other. "Let me guess. You two decided on something."

"We have, Dent," Holly said in a breathless rush. "We've set a date."

That was a momentary sense of loss in Imler's eyes, but he managed a smile, and most of it wasn't pretense. "Ah now," he said. "Isn't that fine?" He pumped Matt's hand and hugged Holly. "That won't be too long away. Things are really moving for you, aren't they, Matt?"

"They did after you pulled me out, Dent. The spring's dug out and running again, and the damaged pipe is relaid. Just because I don't say it every time I see you doesn't mean that I'm not grateful."

Imler grinned. "Thank God for that. I got tired of listening to you."

"Matt thinks he can sell water for five cents a gallon," Holly said. "Won't that excite the town?"

"It will," Imler said absently.

Holly studied him. Something was troubling him. "I thought that would overwhelm you. What is it, Dent?" she asked quietly. "Are you disappointed in us?"

Imler made a quick gesture, wiping out even the suggestion of what she questioned. "Lord, no. Don't you think I could see it coming? What could be happening in town is bothering me."

Matt's eyes sharpened. "What is it, Dent?"

"It's shaping up like race trouble," Imler said bluntly. "It's been growing the past week. Last night, a dozen drunks beat a couple of Chinese senseless. The night before, four Chinese got their queues cut off. I know all of the unemployment is at the basis of it, but it's almost like somebody is guiding it."

"Who?"

Imler wearily shook his head. "I wish I knew. I'd stop it as quick as I'd tromp on a snake." He stared across the

142

room. "It looks like it's all directed at the Chinese, and it could turn into a race riot. I know that the Chinese are a mild race, and they'll take a lot of abuse. But any man will take just so much of that, then he turns. Have you ever been through a race riot, Matt? It's a form of madness that filters into a man's head, turning him against another man because his skin isn't the same color. Its only aim is to destroy and kill, and if it blows up in this town, there won't be much of Candelaria left. If it happens, you won't have much reason to finish your pipeline."

"The fools," Matt said. "Is Ts'ai still here?"

Holly nodded, and worry was deep in her eyes. "Why do you want to see her?"

"I think she should stay here until this trouble dies," Matt said flatly. "But more I want to know where Lo Yen lives. He came in with me tonight."

Holly called Ts'ai, and she came into the room.

She knows, Matt thought. The knowledge of it shadowed her eyes. "Ts'ai, do you know where Lo Yen lives?"

"There is more trouble?" she cried, and the shadows in her eyes came alive and ugly.

"No trouble," Matt assured her. "But we just want to make sure it doesn't happen. Will your son be all right, if you don't go after him tonight? Holly wants you to stay here."

"He will be all right," Ts'ai said in a small, shaking voice. "I have heard of many bad things happening."

"We want to prevent more of them," Matt said gently. "Where does Lo Yen live?"

She gave him directions, and he nodded. "I want him to go back to camp and stay until this is over."

It did not erase the terror in her eyes, but she said, "That will be good."

Holly went with her back to the kitchen, and Matt turned toward the front door. "Tell Holly I'll be back as soon as I can."

"We'll have to tell her before we go," Imler said. "Damnit. Did you think you were going alone."

He raised his voice. "Holly, come in here."

She came back, and indignation was written all over her face. "The poor thing is frightened to death. Why do men have to be such beasts?"

"I guess it's a streak in all of us," Matt said in a tired voice. "Every now and then it has to crop out."

"Wait a minute for me, Matt." Imler left the room, and Matt fretted while he waited.

Imler came back carrying a shotgun and two pistols. He handed the shotgun to Holly. "It's loaded. You know how to use it. Don't let anybody in this house unless it's Matt or me. I don't care who it is. Blast him down, then ask questions."

Her face was pale, but her hands didn't tremble as she took the shotgun from him. "You think there will be trouble?"

"Who can tell what's in those idiots' minds?" Imler said savagely. He handed one of the pistols to Matt. "Just a precaution, Matt."

Matt nodded and thrust the pistol into his waistband. He hadn't brought one with him. Who would have thought that one was needed? A pistol would do much effective arguing against fools than words.

Holly walked to the door with them, and Imler said, "Lock this door, Holly. And the back one, too." He thought he read dissent in her face, for his voice sharpened. "Do you hear me?"

"I hear you," she said quietly.

Imler checked Matt until he heard the click of the lock. "We can go now."

The town seemed quiet enough when they first entered the business district. But on several corners, men were clustered in small groups.

"I don't like that," Imler said blackly.

"You can't stop them from talking, Dent."

That didn't ease the blackness on Imler's face. "I just don't like the way they're doing it. It used to be when a man

144

wanted to talk, he went into a saloon. Why are they standing out here?"

"I don't know, Dent." There was an electric tenseness in the air, and he could feel it crackle against his nerve ends. He didn't see any trouble, but that didn't mean it wasn't coming. In those groups of men he had noticed one significant thing; not one of them was Chinese. And no Chinese were on the streets.

They walked another block, and just around the corner ahead of them he heard muffled swearing and the scuffling of rapid movement.

He threw a glance at Imler. Maybe that trouble was here. He broke into a run, and Imler pounded after him.

They turned the corner, and he would say a good twenty men were just ahead. They formed a rough circle, and he saw the piston-like movement of their legs as they kicked at something. Several of them bent and beat at something on the ground, and their cursing was clear and plain now.

The wall of men prevented him from seeing what they kicked and beat at, but he wouldn't need a second guess.

"Hold it," he yelled and ran harder.

They didn't hear him, or didn't want to. He pulled the gun from his waistband as he ran. He would not try to make them listen to him, but they would pay attention to the pistol.

Between the milling legs he caught glimpses of this mob's target. The number of them, trying to get at that target probably saved the downed men a worse beating. Three Chinese were down, one of them quite still, the other two balled up tightly, their arms wrapped around their heads to protect them.

"Break it up," Matt roared as he reached the outside of the circle. If they heard him, they paid no attention, and his rage spilled over. He chopped with the barrel at a head just before him, and the man dropped without an outcry. He stepped over the limp form. He slashed with the gun

145

barrel at other faces and heads within reach, and he cleared a little space.

"Do you hear me?" he yelled furiously. His rage and the sight of the gun had its effect, and they retreated sullenly before him. The rest of the circle was finally aware of the interruption, and they pulled away from the figures on the ground.

"What are you?" one of them hooted at Matt. "A damned Chink lover?"

Other voices picked it up. "It's that damned Norborne. Hell yes, he's one. He hires them."

Imler stepped through the opened passage and joined Matt. The second drawn gun had its additional effect, and the mob retreated another step.

"Watch them, Dent," Matt said. He glanced at the Chinese. Two of them were sitting up. They seemed well enough though mauled and battered. He stooped over the prone figure. "Just unconscious," he said, looking up at Imler.

He did not waste time trying to talk to the Chinese. He waved at the unconscious man, indicating the other two were to pick him up.

They understood what he meant, and they scrambled to their feet.

"We ain't going to let them turn those Chinks loose?" a voice yelled. "There's only two of them. I say rush them."

Matt searched the semi-ring of faces until he located the speaker. He wasn't surprised to see that it was Hige Barrett. His kind were always found in situations like this.

He jabbed the gun in the direction of Hige Barrett. "You do that, Hige. I'd like nothing better."

The two Chinese had lifted the unconscious man and were moving slowly toward Matt, their eyes rolling fearfully.

"Get him out of here," Matt yelled.

They might not have understood the words, but they certainly understood his tone. They picked up speed, and Matt

146

moved to let them pass. His eyes followed them. While they weren't running, they weren't losing any time, either.

An outraged howl rose from the mob, and now its venom was all directed at Matt and Imler. It had pulled closer together, and it was hovering on the edge of a decision.

"I say rush them," Hige Barrett yelled again.

Matt focused all his attention on him. "Do it," he begged.

Imler gave him a tight-lipped grin. "Don't encourage them," he said dryly.

"You damned animals," Matt raged. "It took this many of you to beat three helpless Chinese. Try it on us."

"You can't get all of us," Barrett bawled.

Matt's gun covered him. "Maybe not. But I'll sure get you. And quite a few more. We can pile you up pretty good. Come on, come on. What's holding you back?"

He had pointed out a fact that most of them had overlooked; two pistols could take quite a toll. The belligerence was beginning to seep out of them. They looked uncertainly at each other, and their feet shuffled up the dust. A few of them, in the rear ranks, were beginning to edge away.

"This ain't over yet, Norborne," Barrett yelled. "We'll get those three along with every damned Chink in town. Maybe we'll include you two."

"You figure on that," Matt said.

By his tone, Imler thought Matt was going to explode, and he put a restraining touch on Matt's arm. "Easy, easy," he murmured.

Matt had been pushed beyond his limit. "Get out of here," he roared. "I won't tell you again." He fired a shot at Barrett's feet, and it geysered dirt on his boots. The men jumped back and put a weak look on each other. They weren't going to support Barrett. Already, they were moving backward. They broke up in fragments and filtered away in different directions.

"You just wait," Barrett yelled again before he disappeared around a corner.

147

"Something knocked the argument out of them," Imler said and chuckled dryly. "I'm telling you, I was sweating."

Matt could admit to that, but his anger hadn't abated. "The stupid bastards. Do you think Barrett stirred up all this?"

"I doubt if he has the mentality," Imler replied. "But I agree with you. Somebody's behind it."

Matt had to find Lo Yen now; he had to tell him to stay off the streets tonight.

Duncan was coming out of Lily's as Matt and Imler passed it. He fell into step with them and asked, "Where are you going?"

"It isn't hard to tell where you've been," Imler said.

"I wasn't trying to hide it," Duncan said cheerfully. He looked at Matt's grim expression and asked, "You been in some kind of trouble."

Matt filled him in with the details, and Duncan said decisively, "I'm going with you. Hell, ain't three better than two?"

Matt had no argument against that. "Come on," he said, and quickened his stride.

Ts'ai's directions were good, for Lo Yen opened the door to Matt's knock. If he was surprised to see Matt here, it didn't show on his face.

Over Lo Yen's shoulder, Matt could see nine or ten men gathered in the front room. He had interrupted some kind of party, and he quickly changed that. If it was some kind of a social gathering, where were the women? And Lo Yen's face said there was nothing festive about this.

"There's been trouble down town, Lo Yen," Matt said. "Dent and I busted up a bunch of men beating three Chinese."

Somebody in the room understood English, for Matt heard the quick outburst of exchange from the men behind Lo Yen. He did not have to understand the Chinese words passed between them to know how they were reacting.

He suddenly knew what this gathering was; a war party,

148

meeting to discuss what they could do about just such happenings he spoke about.

This had to be broken up, just as the mob had been broken up, and he asked, "Aren't you going to ask us in, Lo Yen?"

Lo Yen's expression showed that he didn't want to.

"Damnit," Matt said. "We're doing the best we can to help you."

Lo Yen gave way reluctantly. He introduced Matt and Imler and Duncan to the other men in the room. Matt noticed that none of them offered to shake hands. All of the names were strange to him.

"I'll take you back to camp tonight, Lo Yen," Matt said. "The streets are dangerous tonight for Chinese to be out on them."

Stubbornness stamped Lo Yen's face. "I do not go. My wife and children are here. Are not the streets dangerous for them, too?"

Matt sighed. He had no argument against that. "Then stay off of the streets. Don't go out for any reason. I'll be by for you in the morning."

A pock-marked man stepped forward. "I am Hai Ling," he said. He wasn't an imposing man, but he had a dignity, particularly when he spoke. "Is that how you help us?" he asked bitterly. "Tell us to hide like frightened dogs? Was tonight any different than the nights before it, or the nights that will come?"

Heads behind him bobbed in agreement, and Matt heard their muttered approval.

"Is hiding your solution to the evil that fills men's heart at nights?" Hai Ling went on. "We do not accept your solution. We are men, not dogs. We have taken all the abuse we are going to take."

The approving outbreak was stronger.

"Have you got a better idea?" Matt snapped.

"I know this," Hai Ling answered. "The time for our

149

running has passed. We have trusted the white man before. It has not worked."

Matt was getting angry at this hardheadedness. He said to Imler and Duncan, "We're wasting our time. Let's go."

Lo Yen walked with them to the door. "I am sorry," he said softly. He wasn't apologizing for what Hai Ling said; he was only sorry that it had happened.

"Sure," Matt said curtly. He walked a dozen steps in silence. "They've been pushed about as far as they can be pushed."

Imler nodded. "Who can blame them? This town is ready to blow up."

"Who's this Hai Ling?" Duncan asked.

Matt shook his head. "He apparently has some standing with his people. Didn't you noticed how they listened to him."

His face didn't lighten as both of them nodded. This could drive a thinking man crazy. Hai Ling wouldn't send out those men to be aggressors. But they had taken their last backward step.

He walked along, the scowl deepening on his face. "I think we'd better talk to as many influential white men as we can tomorrow. The merchants will be the ones to start with. If a full-fledged riot breaks out, their stores could suffer a lot of damage. If the damned fools think of burning, those stores can go up in smoke."

"We're not going back to camp tomorrow?" Duncan asked.

"No," Matt said. He wasn't leaving town with this hanging over his head.

CHAPTER TWENTY

Stockton looked up from a crate he was opening before his hardware store. He greeted them cordially enough, but Matt thought a veil obscured his eyes. He supposed it was because of him. There had never been good feeling between them.

"Have you heard about the trouble, Stockton?" he asked.

Stockton pried at another board with a pinch bar, and its nails wailed as they came loose. "I heard about it. How could a man help it? Every morning, there's more talk about what happened last night."

"How do you feel about it?"

"I think those damned heathens are behind it. They're trying to get a white man's job, to run him out of town."

"Oh Jesus," Matt said in disgust. "Have you been trying to stamp down that talk, or encourage it?"

Stockton flushed at the censure in Matt's words. "I'm not going against my own race," he said doggedly.

"Have you ever thought of what can happen if a race riot breaks out?" Matt hammered at him. "People turn into mobs, and they go crazier by the minute. All they want to do then is to destroy. Somebody yells, 'Burn it down,' and it's the only thought left in their heads. It could happen to your store."

Stockton blanched, and Matt said, "I'd think about it."

So far, Imler and Duncan hadn't said a word, and Matt thought their silence was agreement with him. He nodded to Stockton and walked away.

"What do you think, Dent?" he asked.

"You went at him pretty hard, but maybe he needed a jolt like that."

"Are you saying go easier?"

151

"It's a thought, Matt. If you try to get a man to agree with you, don't argue with him. We're trying to make men think, not alienate them. Maybe all we need is to point out what could happen to them."

Duncan didn't speak, but he was nodding.

Stockton's yell checked them, and they turned. Stockton had both clenched fists in the air, and he screamed, "By God, they're not going to burn my store."

Matt shook his head in weary resignation. "There's your answer from him. He's already placed the blame. But maybe you're right, Dent."

He grinned painfully, "From now on, I won't try to club people down. I'll just try to make them see reason."

"Good," Imler said quietly. "We'll get faster coverage, if we split up. You take one side of the street. Duncan and I will take the other. We want to be sure we talk to every merchant in town."

"Maybe you two will do better with your half," Matt said wryly.

Imler laughed, and Duncan grinned. "Somebody's got to help them keep their heads, Matt," Imler said.

Matt went from store to store on his side of the street. He tried to use logic, instead of letting them think they were damned fools not to listen to him. At the end of the business district, he wasn't sure of where he stood. Some of them came out plainly and agreed with him that it had to be stopped. He had some against him, standing on the argument that the yellow-skins had to be driven out of town. A few remained in the wavering class. They would have to see how it turned out before they made a decision.

He crossed the street and joined Imler and Duncan. Both of them had about the same percentage to report. "At least we can make up a list of names we can count on," he said. "That gives us a start."

They nodded solemnly, for they had no better plan.

Matt pointed at a group of men on the corner ahead. It was early for them to gather. He could take a bleak solace that none of them were merchants. "Maybe there's still a hope that some of the sane heads will act." He took a deep breath. "I'm scared, Dent."

"What do you think I am?" Imler asked.

2

Holden tried to keep his impatience from showing. The Barretts were half drunk, and they were in a surely, mean mood.

"I thought you boys were men of action," he said. "But the way it's going—" He let a shrug finish for him.

"We haven't been sitting on our hands," Hige snarled.

Holden's laugh had a sneer in it. "What have you accomplished? You've beat up a few Chinks. That's not driving them out of town."

Holden didn't let his annoyance show on his face. He would have to spend more time and more money on whiskey.

"I thought you two had some influence in town. I thought you could make it see it your way."

Hige said a vicious oath. "They were listening to us until that damned Sadler stepped in. He's advising them that violence isn't the answer. He's got them to believing they'll lose more than they stand to gain."

"Sadler, eh?" Holden said softly. He would never have picked Sadler to be one of the level heads. "Maybe I can talk some sense into him."

Their expressions said they didn't think he could, and it aroused Holden's anger. Maybe he couldn't do anything by talking, but he didn't want them to know. He already had proof of Sadler's hardheadedness. But there were other ways.

"I'll see you later," he said and walked out.

He looked around town until he located Sadler. Then he followed the man for a couple of hours and could never catch the man alone. Every place Sadler went, men joined him, and Holden fumed until their talk was over. He had to keep a grip on his nerves. Surely, sometime during the afternoon, Sadler would be alone.

He was beginning to believe it was hopeless when Sadler turned toward the livery stable. And he was alone.

Holden quickened his stride. "Hold it a minute, Sadler. I want to talk to you."

Sadler turned, and his cheeks tightened. "We haven't got anything to talk about," he said coldly.

Holden glanced around. After those maddening hours, he could see nobody near Sadler. What he had in mind was a risk, but it might not come again for a long time.

"I hear you're protecting the Chinks," he said.

"I've got nothing to love them for," Sadler said slowly. "But it's senseless to tear up a town because I don't like the color of their skin." He remembered he was supposed to have nothing to say to Holden, and he clamped his lips together, and started to turn away.

Holden's hand closed on the gun in his pocket and let Sadler get a step away. He couldn't risk a shot, and he wished he had something heavier than the barrel of this gun.

He jerked the gun out and reversed the butt. "I'm not through with you," he said and struck Sadler across the head.

It was a vicious blow, and the sound of its striking sounded like an overripe melon being dropped on a hard surface. Sadler made a gargled groan, and his eyes rolled up into his head. He fell limply as though not a bone in his body supported him.

Holden breathed hard as he looked all around. His breathing eased. As far as he could tell nobody had seen that blow. He looked down at the wound in the back of Sadler's skull. It looked all caved in, and blood gushed out of it.

Holden bent over him. The man's color was a cold gray, and he could detect no sign of breathing.

Holden forced himself to remain calm. He could wait a few more minutes to be sure. He closely watched the lips,

154

and he could see no fluttering of life in them. The one blow had done it; he could be sure now.

He straightened and dropped the gun into his pocket. "Help," he yelled. He drew a deep breath for a more vigorous effort. "Help, somebody."

His voice must have carried well, for a block down the street he saw a man step out of a store. He looked in Holden's direction, gesticulated, and said something that Holden couldn't hear. He started at a dead run toward Holden, and two other rushed out of the store behind him.

Holden's voice, or the activity, pulled more attention his way. All along the street people were coming out of doors and running toward him.

"Help," he yelled again, though the additional call wasn't necessary.

He breathed in agitated breaths as they reached him. He pointed at the body in the dust. "Sadler," he said. "I'm afraid he's dead."

One of the men leaned over Sadler and put his ear close to Sadler's mouth. "Dead, all right," he agreed. "What happened?"

He had to convince them, and Holden didn't think that would be hard. As wrought up as this town was men were ready to believe anything."

"He was a half-block ahead of me," he said. "Two Chinese came out of nowhere. They jumped him. It startled me so much that I froze for a moment. God forgive me."

Those eyes were hardening, but it wasn't at him. "Go on," one of them said.

"They struck him down with a club. I yelled at them, and they ran. I wish to God I had had a gun. I tried to catch them, but it was useless." His voice picked up a sorrowful note that censured himself. "When I came back, Sadler was dead. I wish I could have done something about it."

The watchers broke into an outraged babble of talk. "The goddamned Chinese," one of them said. "Didn't I say we waited too long to drive them out? By God, it's getting pretty

155

bad when a white man can't walk the streets without being afraid for his life."

Heads bobbed all around him in violent agreement. "You didn't know them?" they asked Holden.

"Who can tell them apart?" Holden replied. "I'll help you with poor Sadler."

"Naw, Mr. Holden. We'll take care of him."

He didn't mind being recognized now. "If there's anything I can do—" He let it fade away and walked away.

That would do it, he thought in triumph. Let the Barrett brothers say now that men wouldn't listen to them. It would be dark in another hour, and he would say it would happen tonight. Men couldn't contain their inflamed feelings any longer.

CHAPTER TWENTY-ONE

Shotguns were under Matt's, Imler's, and Duncan's arms as they walked down the street. Matt hadn't seen any alarming gatherings as yet, but it wasn't quite dark. What had Hai Ling said? Something about the evil in men's hearts being released by the darkness. He could be right. Several times Matt had heard cries, too far away to distinguish words. They had investigated a few of them, and so far, had found nothing.

"Do you think they'll be out on the streets, Matt?" Duncan asked.

Matt cocked his head, listening. A mob did not move in stealth. If something broke out, he would hear it. "Too many, I'm afraid. Maybe others will think it over and decide discretion is the better course. I hope to God some of them get their doors kicked in." He didn't want trouble to break out, but he could feel it coming. It had the heavy, oppressive quality of air that suddenly had gone too still before the onslaught of a heavy storm.

"Man's an awesome animal," Imler said and sighed.

Matt gave him a bleak grin. "He is. Sometimes, I don't know how God can stand them."

"Just pray He doesn't lose his patience," Imler said.

Matt was disappointed with the number of men, waiting in Arnold's store. Thirteen men were here, and he had expected, no, he changed that, had thought that at least double that number would be here. They thought he was right and had taken his advice, for all of them carried shotguns. A shotgun could change the mind of the most determined mob.

Their faces were strained, and he held up a hand at the outbreak of talk directed at him.

"It's been quiet so far, Matt," one of them said.

"I hope it stays that way," he answered. "Has anybody seen any crowds on the streets?"

He got negative words and shakes of heads in answer. "We've got to keep it from happening. We'll split up in groups of four. If we run across any bunches, order them to get off the streets."

That sounded like a gulp before the following words came. "What if they don't pay any attention to us, Matt?"

"Damnit," he said savagely. "That's why you're carrying those shotguns. Blast a hole in them. I don't give a damn what color they are."

He saw the tight looks they gave each other. "Do you want them running over you?" he demanded.

They didn't, but they weren't happy about the alternative that faced them.

"Dent, go with them." He named three men. He and Duncan would go with another bunch. He hoped that his and Imler's and Duncan's presence would stiffen backbones. He could only pray that the other two bunches were tough enough.

They filed out of the store, shotguns under their arms. Matt paused for final instructions. "If any of you hear a shotgun get over to the sound as fast as you can." He didn't add that some of them might need fast and efficient help; they should know that.

He watched three groups move off in different directions.

"Looks like we've got a lot of walking to do tonight," Duncan said.

Matt frowned at him. Nothing ever bothered Duncan. Matt just hoped he could depend as much on the other two.

They spread out from him and walked slowly down the street. Duncan had called it right. They would patrol the streets until the dawn ended the night. The damned waiting for something to happen was harder than the action, itself.

Four heads swiveled in all directions, looking for something they couldn't see. Matt cursed the darkness and the

158

unusual silence. A normal night had some sound. There was nothing now, no traffic, no voices.

This is what you wanted, isn't it? he asked himself. Yes, but not with this much weight, he thought wryly.

He heard a lot of voices then, all bunched together as though a furious argument had suddenly broken out. It sounded as though it came from two streets over. It broke the silence all right, but this was what he had been dreading. This was the voice of a mob.

Three faces turned toward him, and he shook his head. He had sent Imler over that way, and Imler should be closer than they were. He could wait a few minutes longer.

The volume increased, rising in shrill pitch as though men screamed at each other. He frowned as he tried to pick out individual words. He didn't like it. That sounded like two sets of language being hurled at each other. If that was right, it meant that a bunch of Chinese were on the street, in confrontation with white men.

"Let's go," he yelled and broke into a run. He hadn't taken a half-dozen strides before he heard the booming report of a shotgun. He shouldn't have waited, thinking that Imler could handle it. Besides, Imler could have been pulled in another direction. Matt's indecision had cost him time. He heard the heavy report of another shotgun shell. My God, it sounded like open warfare, and he could visualize Imler, or one of the other patrols being overwhelmed.

He raced down the street, turned a corner, and wild chaos was before him. He didn't know how many were locked in battle, but every place he looked he saw men struggling. Just as he arrived three men overwhelmed a slighter figure, and a Chinese slumped to the ground. This couldn't have lasted long, but already a dozen figures were down in the street. They fought with their bare hands, with sticks and clubs, and Matt was only fearful that guns and knives would appear.

Imler ran up to him, and his face was frantic.

"That your shotgun I heard?" Matt snapped.

159

"I fired into the air. They didn't pay any attention to it. I don't think they even heard it."

Matt swore, and part of it was directed at Imler. "I told you to drop some of them."

Imler was miserably tense. "I was working up to it, Matt. Every time I pulled down on some of them, something stopped me."

Matt gave him a bitter look. He knew how Imler felt, but that wouldn't stop this madness.

He fired one barrel over their heads, and that didn't stop them. He could appreciate Imler's reluctance; he didn't want to kill any of those fools, struggling in the street, but the cost of a few lives here could save many more later on. Still, he aimed the second barrel at their legs and pulled the trigger. He caught a cluster of them in his pattern, and a half-dozen men dropped to the ground, rolling in the dust and yelling their pain.

That broke up the fighting. Men pulled apart, seeking their own kind. Matt saw many a bloody spot on white and yellow skin.

He glared at them as he thumbed fresh loads into the shotgun. "I'll kill every one of you, if I have to," he said furiously. He was glad to see that his other two patrols had arrived. Maybe the sight of that many shotguns would drive some sense into their heads.

"Break it up," he yelled. "Get off of the street." He swore at these two bunches under his breath. They weren't budging.

"Drive them off the street," he instructed his patrols. "If they won't move, break their heads."

They advanced in a line, driving the rioters before them. He heard the groaning of wounded men as he passed them and felt no pity. They had asked for it.

The mob, in two segments, retreated sullenly before that steady advance. But they were in no mood yet to listen to reason, or anything else. They hooted and catcalled at Matt

160

and his men, and his face flamed at some of the names they called at him.

A rock was suddenly hurled from one of the bunches, and it grazed Matt's shoulder. That could be the opening of a barrage of anything they could get their hands on. Momentarily, the two groups, had united in a solid front against the men who had tried to save them.

A piece of wood flew through the air and struck Duncan in the face. He staggered, and Matt thought he was going down. He flung an arm about him, supporting Duncan until the dizziness passed.

Blood was on Duncan's face. He touched fingers to it, looked at the stain and asked plainitively, "Didn't I look bad enough without this?"

"Rush them," Matt yelled, goaded beyond endurance.

The mob broke and scattered in all directions before the charge. It became a footrace between individuals, and Matt saw that by chasing them, he was losing the advantage of a united force.

"Hold it, hold it," he yelled, recalling them. He stared in baffled rage at the retreating rioters. The damned idiots. He was trying to save them from their madness, and they would have no part of it.

He waited until the men pulled back to him and said, "We've got hurt men on our hands. See what can be done for them."

It had been a short brawl but a costly one. He counted a dozen men down, and half of that number was due to him. He knew not the slightest remorse. If it happened again, he hoped he could put every damned one of them down.

He approached a Chinese bending over another one stretched out on the ground. "Is he hurt bad?" he asked gruffly.

Hai Ling looked up at him. "He was knocked unconscious. He recovers now. Two of them jumped him at once."

The man on the ground stirred, mumbled something and, with the help of Hai Ling's arm, managed to sit up.

Matt looked at him in outrage. Lo Yen sat there, shaking his head to clear its dizziness.

"I didn't expect to find you in this," Matt said flatly.

Even beaten and disheveled, Lo Yen still had his dignity. "Why not?" he asked. "These are my people. We did not make the fight. It was pushed on us."

"Did this help your wife and children?" Matt snapped.

Lo Yen would not look at him.

"He only did what had to be done," Hai Ling said flatly.

Matt fought the temptation to bash in both of their heads. It was hopeless, trying to reach men in a mood like this, but he made one more effort. "Keep your people off of the street. I promise you I'll get the other element under control."

"You would have him hide like dogs," Hai Ling jeered.

That did it, that tore the lid off of Matt's restraint. "From now on, I'm going to break every head I see involved. Regardless of his color."

Hai Ling shrugged. "It is no more than we expected." He was tough and seasoned by abuses; Matt couldn't stare him down.

"Some of your people are hurt," Matt said curtly. "Get them off of the street."

He and Hai Ling were on the same errand of mercy, but it didn't make them brothers. They patched and bound up, and helped support the men who could walk away. Those wounded by the shotgun pellets needed far more attention. The doctors were going to have a busy night, for Matt had the uneasy feeling that this was only the beginning of it.

He and Imler walked outside after they had helped carry the last wounded man inside the building. Matt wished he had time to get a cup of coffee, to sit down with it and just stare blankly into space with nothing picking at his mind.

"Maybe it knocked some sense into their heads, Matt," Imler said.

Matt remembered the sorrowful decision that he had seen in Hai Ling's eyes. "It won't," he said flatly. "Hai Ling accepts the worst as being inevitable. And the whites want it."

He threw up his hands in a fatalistic gesture. "Sadler's killing really inflamed them. They're going to pay back every single Chinese in Candelaria."

"Do you think the Chinese really killed him, Matt?"

Matt stared broodingly down the street. "I wish I knew." He sighed and asked, "Ready to go?" It was time to regroup with the others and start out again. He was afraid a long and fruitless night stretched out before them.

CHAPTER TWENTY-TWO

Matt split his force into half, abandoning the division he had originally used. It meant that he couldn't cover the town as thoroughly, but it would also save his men from being overwhelmed by sheer numbers.

Sporadic fighting broke out over town, and a man can only cover so much ground. Matt would hear an outbreak and run for it, and by the time he reached the scene, the combatants had fled, leaving wounded and battered men unable to run away. It was maddening trying to cope with these hit and run affairs. Every time, Matt stooped to do what he could for the hurt, fighting broke out in other parts of town. He administered to broken heads and torn flesh, and in three cases, picked up dead men.

He wasn't making any progress in keeping the town controlled, and it was driving him wild.

He and Duncan carried in another customer for one of the doctors, and Matt scowled at the blood on his hands. The man had been bleeding pretty bad. "Damned if I don't think I'll just pull out and leave them go at each other. That would eventually end it." It would through sheer attrition, though it would cut a bloody swath.

Duncan shook his head in that familiar, stubborn gesture. "But you won't do that. Though I'm agreeing with you that right now it looks hopeless. We arrest some of the Chinese and some of the whites. We lock them up in different buildings, and the fighting seems to grow worse. It's like dipping out the ocean with a teaspoon. Matt, if we could only get to the leaders."

"I've been looking for Hai Ling and Lo Yen," Matt said. "I don't think the Barretts are leading the whites." He scowled down the street. He had seen the Barrett brothers a couple of times, but they had been too fast for him to corner. He suspected they had a big hand in this, but who was behind them? It took a stronger mind than the Barretts had to lead this. He had one small consolation. So far, the Chinese and whites had fought each other. But they hadn't turned to destruction and burning. He was afraid that consolation wouldn't last long. It would happen, and he was surprised to see that it hadn't occurred up to now.

"Matt, I saw some of the merchants running with the whites."

"Yes," Matt half-shouted. "Goddamn them." He knew what would happen, if the destruction started. That would take the merchants' minds off of the fighting. He almost wished it would. He had warned them about it, and they hadn't listened.

Matt whipped his head about at a new outbreak of sound. That sounded as though it came from little Chinatown. He thought he saw a pinkish cast in the sky above it, and it slowly changed to a lurid red.

"There it goes," he cried. Now all hell would break loose. He ran toward the scene, and Duncan and the others ran after him. Now they had two things to fight; man and fire.

2

Holden wasn't satisfied with the way things were going. Breaking a few Chinese heads might suit the Barretts; it didn't him.

Hige and Coe Barrett were having a fine time. Hige tilted a bottle up to his mouth, and some of it ran out of his lip corner, diluting the blood caked there. It ran down his chin in a pinkish stream.

"By God, there won't be a Chink left in town by the time we've through," he crowed.

"If Norborne doesn't stop you first," Holden snapped. A couple of times he had seen Norborne and ducked back just

165

in time to prevent being seen. He had to do something to draw Norborne to one spot and hold his attention there.

"We can get at the little monkeys faster," he said. He had their interest, but it wasn't favorable. They thought he was going to call off the fighting. "We ought to start burning down some of their houses. If we do that, they won't come slinking back when we drive them out of town. They won't have anything to return to."

They shouted their approval, and it gave him a sense of power. He held them in his hand, and he could mold them any way he chose.

"Some of you get some torches," he said. "And bring back a few containers of kerosene."

"I've got it," Neilson said eagerly and turned and raced down the street.

Holden watched him go with derisive eyes. The damned fool would get those items out of his store. Holden wanted to see his face when the torches he supplied were put to his store.

Neilson brought back a half-dozen torches, and their light cast a murky, flickering reflection over men's faces. A good thirty men followed Holden down the street, and he kept alert eyes out for Norborne. He did not want to come up against him; not with that shotgun in his hands.

Two Chinese came around the corner toward them, and the men behind Holden started to break after them.

Holden threw up his arm, stopping them. He watched the Chinese with amused eyes. The two men were a tempting target, but he was after something bigger now.

"No," he said sharply, checking the growling. "We'll round up all of them later."

His eyes remained on the running figures. They scuttled like little, frightened rabbits. Soon, he would have every Chinese in town doing the same thing.

He stopped the restless stirring behind him. "We're not looking for Chinks now." Another outbreak of fighting would pull Norborne quicker than anything else.

166

He picked an isolated house at the edge of Chinatown, and Holden saw no Chinese around. The door was locked, and he kicked it in. A cowering woman and two children huddled in a corner.

He threw out both arms, holding back the men from surging in. "Just throw them out," he ordered. "That's enough."

The men handled the woman and children roughly, throwing them out into the street. He heard the woman's and children's whimpering. It didn't turn him. After the abuse he had suffered at Chinese hands, a few tears wouldn't arouse his pity.

It was a poor, shabby hut with few furnishings. "Pile everything in the center," he directed. A few men picked up some small items and started to carry it outside.

"What are you going to do with that?" Holden demanded.

That pulled surprised looks from him. "Why, take it," one of them replied.

"That junk," he said contemptuously. "I'll show you where to get something worth taking. Put it on the pile."

They reluctantly tossed the items on the pile, and Holden doused a container of kerosene on it, then applied a torch.

It caught right now, and Holden's eyes glistened as he looked at the leaping flames. Nothing could stop it now. He whirled and darted for the door.

They wanted to stand around and watch it, and he shook his head. They had time to burn another hovel before the flames pulled Norborne here.

The second hut added to the red glow that was filling the sky. He thought he heard yells in the distance. It was time to leave.

"Split up," he ordered. "We'll meet at the head of the business district." His success made him drunk with triumph. Now he was going to see what he wanted; he was going to see Candelaria burn down.

"We could run into Norborne there," one of them objected.

The man was wrong. Norborne couldn't get there until the fire was started. "Not until we burn down a few stores," he

167

said. "Didn't I promise that I'd show you things that are worth carrying off?"

"You're going to burn down the stores?" Neilson squalled in dismay. "Why one of them could be my store."

"It could be," Holden said sardonically.

He led them down a side street. A man, behind him, looked around and said, "Hey, Neilson and a couple of others are slipping away."

It tickled Holden to think of those men following the wrong men. "Let them. It won't do them any good."

Behind him, the sky was much redder, and he heard screams in both outrage and terror.

"That'll keep them busy for some time," he said and quickened his step. He would add to the red glow in the sky that would keep the whole damned town busy.

3

Two houses were burning fiercely by the time Matt and Duncan reached the scene. Imler came pounding up from the opposite direction. The first was already fire-weakened, and it threatened to collapse at any moment. The second would follow soon.

The third house was threatened by the heat, and Matt thought he saw its roof smoking. It wasn't inconceivable that the entire district would go up in flames.

The Chinese were gathered in a purposeless group, and Matt heard their wailing and lamentations. A few made individual effort to save something, and they ran into and out of houses like ants with no leader. That might save a few items; it wouldn't save the district.

Matt saw Hai Ling and Lo Yen, and their faces were heavy with sullen dismay. They made no sound, but their shoulders slumped in bitter defeat.

"Standing around wringing your hands, won't do you any good," Matt said.

Hai Ling looked at him with bitter, hating eyes. "What

168

can we do? There is no water. You can tell us that? After it was burned by white men." The hostility of his manner pulled attention this way, and Chinese edged toward Matt and Duncan. They hated too now, and a wrong word or a wrong move could spill it out all over them.

"Stand around and moan about it, or do something to save your houses," Matt snapped.

Lo Yen's head raised, and a hope was in his eyes. He had worked for this man for a long while. He had seen this man solve many problems.

"What can we do without water?"

Matt grinned at him. The old relationship was back. "There's nothing we can do about the burning houses. And the third one will go at any minute." A rise in the pitch of the crowd's voice pulled his head around. The smoking roof had burst into fire, and tongues of flames licked across it. He had called that one right, and he said, "Hai Ling, don't let any more of your people go into that house."

He eyed the house next in line to the burning ones, and he had better move beyond it. He wanted a house torn down to make a gap in the line of fire, and he lacked everything with which to do it. He needed tools; he needed sledges and pinch bars. In its place he had one thing; he had hand power.

He pointed at the house he wanted. "Tear it down."

The people, close enough to hear and understand him, raised a new wailing, and that was stubbornness in Hai Ling's eyes.

"I would rather see a few houses torn down, than to watch all of them burn."

"I would listen to him," Lo Yen advised. "I have never known him to be wrong."

Hai Ling stared at Matt a long moment, then made his decision. "Tear it down. That and the next one to it." He spoke in Chinese then, and Matt imagined he repeated the same instructions.

"Can you get it started, Riley?" Matt asked.

"Sure," Duncan said cheerfully. He walked to the wall

farthest from the fire and hurled his bulk at the flimsy wall. It groaned and gave under the assault, and the entire house shuddered under the impact. Duncan did it again, and boards broke and splintered. A man could get his hands on one of them now.

The Chinese understood what Duncan was doing, and they poured toward him in a willing wave. They had their hands and the weight of their bodies to put against weak walls, but there were many of them. Behind them a woman uttered a shrill cry of distress, higher than any other sound. Another woman would probably be making that same sound before this was over.

The wall began to sway, and the roof sagged with it. It came down with a crash, puffing up dust around it.

"Tell them not to leave any wood to burn," Matt called, and Hai Ling nodded and repeated the words in Chinese.

Matt had heard of the fabled Chinese ability to accomplish impossible tasks with only their hands, and this was a small proof of it. A mass of ants attacked the house, but each of those ants had a pair of hands. They tore at the house and ripped it away board by board. Those two houses came down in an amazingly short time. There was only bare ground where a short while ago, two structures had stood.

They had opened a gap between the burning houses and the others in the row, and the wind was favorable, blowing the flames from the houses as yet untouched.

Matt was debating upon ordering another one to be torn down to increase the fire gap, and somebody grabbed his arm. He turned his head and frowned at Neilson. If he ever saw a distraught man, this was one. Neilson panted too hard for Matt to understand his words.

"Say it slower," he said.

Neilson got a grip on himself, but the harassment remained in his eyes. "I've been looking all over for you. I find you saving something like this?"

"You know of a better fire?" Matt asked in sour humor. Neilson pointed toward the eastern sky. "There!" His face was tragic. "They're burning down the stores. My store is blazing. I tried to stop them, and they knocked me aside." The marks on his face were a mute testimony to rough handling.

"You keep saying they? Who are *they?*" Matt wanted names.

Neilson sucked in a fresh breath. "The Barretts. Gary Holden. Everybody listens to him. I heard him say they would burn down the whole town before he was through."

"Ah," Matt said softly. He had the name he wanted. It was too bad he or Lo Yen hadn't killed the man before. Holden had long earned it.

He called Hai Ling to him and said, "Keep your people watching this fire. If you think it's still going to spread, you know what to do."

That was new respect in Hai Ling's nod. "If you need more help—"

Matt looked at the faces of the Chinese turned toward him. They would do as he said, but this time he needed more than hand power. The stores were substantially built, and mere hand power could not tear them down.

"No, Hai Ling. This will take something different."

"But I go with you," Lo Yen said. "I forgot where my place was before."

Matt grinned at him. "Let's go then." He gathered up his original force and ran toward the increasing fiery hue in the sky.

He didn't have the slightest idea as how to stop this new fire. There was no water; the substantial part of Candelaria could go up before this night was over.

CHAPTER TWENTY-THREE

For an instant, he thought the entire business district was in flames as he turned onto the street. Then he saw that only one side of the street was burning, and the fire hadn't yet extended the entire length of it.

He heard the yelling and saw the black figures of people apparently rushing aimlessly about against the backdrop of the fire. Then he could differentiate between them. The ones at this end of the street were trying to save things from the stores before the fire reached them, and the others, closer to the flames, were nothing but looters, stealing whatever they could get their hands on.

He pointed them out to Imler and Duncan. "Looters," he said harshly.

He lengthened his stride, passing merchants who were frantically trying to save a pitful percentage of their wares.

"Hold it," he yelled as a figure appeared in the smashed-in door of a store.

He heard the shattering crash of another store front, and a new blossom of flame appeared in it. Another store was fired.

The man's arms were laden, and Matt's yell didn't stop him. He ran awkwardly because of his burden, and Matt leveled the shotgun. He would not give the looter another warning.

He pulled the trigger, and the blast of the shotgun sounded loud above the yelling and fire noise. He did not aim for the scissoring legs; he aimed for the back.

The swath of pellets cut the man down, and he broke in the middle of reaching for another stride. Merchandise flew in all directions as he fell. He slid a few feet in the street and was still.

Matt advanced toward him, the second barrel ready. He toed over the figure and said, "Barrett," as he looked at the anguish-frozen face. This was Hige, the older of the two. This was the one that Neilson had named, and Matt only hoped that he had an equal chance at the other one.

The looters heard that shotgun blast, for up and down the street, they ran out of stores. They glanced at Matt, standing over the body, then scurried in the opposite direction. He fired at the closest one to him, and the man might have staggered, but he was too far away for the pellets to do more than sting him.

He wished he could do nothing else but run them down one by one, but he had something far bigger on his hands. He had a fire raging out of control.

Imler joined him and stared at the flames with awe in his face. "Matt, we can't stop that."

"No," Matt agreed. Hands couldn't tear down those stores board by board. Even if they had the proper tools, the time element was gone. The stores were jammed together, and the wind kept the flames leaping from store to store. The only chance of saving the remaining stores on that side of the street was to build a firegap, and that would take far more power than men possessed.

A word flashed into his mind. "Dynamite, Dent. We can blast that fire out of life." Black powder would probably do it too, but it would take more time. He had handled a lot of black powder in his day, but he hadn't handled much dynamite.

He grinned awkwardly at Imler. "I'm kind of green when it comes to dynamite."

Imler's eyes gleamed. "I can handle it, Matt." He was damned grateful he had a younger, more alert mind with him. He hadn't even thought of dynamite. But that would do it; its blast would literally snuff out a fire.

173

"Sikeston got it someplace," Matt said. "Maybe Stockton's has some left."

Stockston's store was near the end of the block, and he was trying to carry his merchandise out into the street. He would carry out an armload, pile it up in the street, then run back for another load.

Matt's grip on his arm stopped him. "We need dynamite. Have you got any?"

"Help me," Stockton pleaded. "I've got to get it out. If I don't, everything in there is going to burn up."

Matt's question hadn't got through to that frantic mind, and he said brutally, "It sure as hell will, if you don't find some dynamite. That's the only chance we've got of stopping it."

For an instant, he thought the man was incapable of comprehension, then Stockton's eyes rounded, and his breathing was faster. "I have some left. It's in the shed back of the store."

"Then you'd better get moving, or watch it burn."

Stockton ran through the store, and Matt followed him. He swore as Stockton fumbled in his pocket for the key to the shed, and Stockton lost more valuable seconds unlocking the padlock.

Matt pushed him aside. A half-dozen cases of dynamite were stacked in a corner at the rear of the shed. He hurried to it and seized the top case. This was all the time they had; if a case wouldn't do it, then this side of the block was gone.

Stockton started to pick up another case, and Matt roared, "This is enough. Bring the fuse."

He carried the case on his shoulder, and with his free hand, picked up a pinch bar as he ran back through the store.

"Good," Imler said as Matt laid it down before him.

Matt ripped off the top boards, and Imler went to work. His hands were dexterous and sure; he knew the value of time as well as Matt did.

He made three sticks into a bundle and fused them, measur-

174

ing out three lengths of fuse before he attached them to the sticks.

"That ought to be enough, Matt."

"I'll take the first store," Matt said. It was next to a store now burning fiercely, and the heat would be intense.

"I'll take the next one," Imler said. He looked around for another volunteer, and men looked uneasily at each other. Dynamite was an awesome thing, and their looks said they were afraid of the stuff.

"Hell," Duncan said. "If you two can do it, I can too. Tell me what you want."

"Just put the sticks inside the store and lay the fuse out until you reach its end. At my signal I want those fuses lit at the same time. Light it then run like hell."

Duncan grinned. "Mister, you just put speed in my feet."

Matt picked up his three sticks of dynamite and the coil of fuse and ran for the store next to the burning one. He did not look at Imler and Duncan, but he could hear the thud of their feet.

He felt the heat as he reached the store, and it seemed to shrivel his skin. He couldn't tell whether or not it had yet caught, but smoke swirled inside it, and he coughed against it. He did not dare draw another breath, for this one seared his lungs. Even if the heat hadn't dried up his mouth, he would have been too scared to spit. He had no idea of what this kind of heat would do to dynamite, and the question was big in his mind; will it blow up in my hand? He ducked his head and darted inside. He wasn't going to linger any longer than was absolutely necessary. He laid the dynamite down, and uncoiling the fuse, he backed out. Imler had cut a good length. It reached to the middle of the street before it ran out.

He could breath more freely out here, and he drew several quick breaths to ease his aching lungs.

It seemed an eternity before he saw Imler and Duncan backing out as they played out their fuses. He bent over

175

and struck a match, shielding its flame with a hand. Imler raised his arm high, then swept it downward.

Not too fast, Matt told himself. If he didn't make it on the first match, it would cost more precious time to strike another match.

He touched the flickering flame to the end of the fuse until it spit sparks. He held it there a moment longer, making this attempt sure. The lighted fuse ran along the ground, spitting out sparks and smoke. Matt turned and ran. All the onlookers had moved back as far as they could, and Matt reached the far edge of the street before he dove for the ground.

It was an agony of waiting, probably magnified many times its true length. A dozen thoughts tormented him; had the fuse gone out, had the dynamite failed to go off? He was tempted to raise his head and look, and he stubbornly held it against the dirt.

Imler must have measured those three lengths of fuse well, and all three matches must have been touched to them at the same time, for the three blasts went off simultaneously, sounding as one. Matt felt the shock of it run through the ground, thumping against his chest. The air was filled with flying debris. A piece of wood hurtled through the air, grazing Matt's shoulder, and beside him he heard a man cry out in sudden pain.

He cautiously lifted his head, and his eyes filled with awe as he looked at the craters that had once been three stores. The burning store, next to them was now out as though a great wind had whipped it into nonexistence. At the far end of the block the fire still burned, but the firegap between it and the remaining stores should stop it.

Imler lay a dozen yards from Matt, and he managed a shaky grin. "It's out." The two words inadequately expressed the relief he felt.

It wasn't quite over; the street was cluttered with shattered boards and what had once been salable items. Some of those things were only smoking, but a few of them had feeble fire stealing along them.

Matt jumped to his feet. "Stamp those fires out," he yelled. It broke the grip shock had had on men, and they stamped out fires like men attacking a den of snakes. Every one of them was grinning. Candelaria wasn't going to burn down; not this night anyway.

Matt didn't see Lo Yen. The last time he remembered seeing him was just before he planted that dynamite.

"Where's Lo Yen?" he asked Duncan.

"He took off right after you ran for the store," Duncan replied. "He said something about seeing that his sister was all right."

Until now, Matt hadn't thought of Holly and Ts'ai, and he cursed himself for it. He doubted that the Imler house was in danger, but Holden still might be around. Who could guess what went through that crazy mind?

He didn't want to alarm Imler, and he said, "Dent, keep an eye on the business district. Arrest or shoot any man you don't think belongs here."

"Where are you going?" Imler asked with quick suspicion.

"I'm just going to check on Chinatown. To be sure the fire is out there."

Imler's suspicion wasn't quite allayed, but he nodded.

CHAPTER TWENTY-FOUR

From the far end of the street Holden saw the dynamite blast snuff out the fire, and he had also seen Hige Barrett shot down. Too many men, who had been following, had seen it too, and they were fleeing madly in all directions. He doubted that he could gather them again, not against Norborne's willingness to use that shotgun, but it didn't matter. He had left his mark on Candelaria, one that would be remembered for a long time. He laughed deep in his throat. He might not have wiped it out, but he had crippled it for a long time.

He had one job to finish, and he headed toward the Imler house. He would never find a better time. He still carried a container of kerosene, and he would have use for it. Holly and that Chinese bitch were probably still in the house, and it did not matter. Both of them had spurned him, then rubbed his nose into the dirt. He had paid back quite a few debts tonight, and this last one would wipe the slate clean.

The lights that were on in the house were clustered in one section of it. The women should be there, and that was where he would start the fire.

He looked all around before he uncapped the container, and he could see nobody. The pungent fumes of the kerosene bit at his nostrils, and he had never smelled anything finer.

He started at the back, moving toward the front, and he splashed the liquid on the wall as he walked. The container would last all of this wall and around in the front. He was so engrossed in his task that he heard nothing until a voice asked, "What do you think you are doing?"

He dropped the container and jumped, momentarily thinking his heart had stopped. He whirled, and his voice lodged in his throat, making nothing but a squeaky sound.

"You," he finally managed to say, and triumph ran in a mighty flow in him. This was the Chinaman who had beaten him, and it made his night full. He clutched the pistol, in his pocket, not drawing it until Lo Yen moved closer.

Lo Yen came a few steps closer to him. "What were you doing here? You were told to stay away. This time—"

"You've just run out of that, you yellow bastard." Holden pulled out the pistol and aimed it at Lo Yen's face. At this distance he could not possibly miss.

2

Matt didn't run, for he didn't think the urgency was that great, but his strides were long and rapid. He checked the loads in the shotgun, and they were fresh ones. My God, he was weary. He could feel the drain of the night, pulling at his legs, and it was effort to keep them moving.

He sighed with relief as he saw the lights in the house. For a moment, he didn't see Lo Yen, and he thought, if he came here, he's probably in the house. He would check and warn Lo Yen not to go off by himself the rest of this night.

He saw the two figures then, standing at one corner of the house, and momentarily, he didn't recognize them. He hurried his stride. They faced each other, and from their attitudes Matt doubted that either of them realized anybody was close.

As he neared them he recognized the smaller figure. Lo Yen! The bigger one was Holden, and Matt didn't yell at him, though he wanted to. That was tension in Holden's figure, and Matt's yell would shatter it.

Holden's hand moved, and when it showed again, a gun was in it. Matt was within shotgun range, but he wasn't going to be in time to stop Holden. He groaned deep in his throat, and threw up the butt to his shoulder. "Holden!"

The name came out hoarse and cracked. He didn't dare risk firing. Lo Yen was within the gun's pattern.

Flame lanced from the gun's muzzle that Holden held, and Lo Yen dropped with the limpness of an empty grain sack.

"You bastard," Matt screamed, and rage sickened him. He pulled one trigger, then the second one, the reports almost sounding as one. Holden was literally blasted off of his feet, and his garbled sound was snapped off before it was fully formed.

Matt ran the remaining yards, and it wouldn't matter now. Even before he looked at Lo Yen he knew nothing would reach him in time.

He didn't put a second look on Holden. Sometimes a man knew without verifying it. He dropped to his knees beside Lo Yen and turned him over. Blood covered Lo Yen's face. Matt had been too late to help Lo Yen.

"Oh goddamnit," he said over and over, and he could think of nothing else.

Cries, from inside the house, reached him, and he straightened stiffly. He didn't want either of the women seeing this.

He caught Holly just as she rushed out of the door. "Don't go any farther," he said wearily.

Her eyes were round with terror, and she gasped, "Matt, I heard shots."

"Keep Ts'ai from coming out," he said and leaned the shotgun against the house.

Thank God she was the kind of a woman who reacted without a barrage of questions.

She swept his face with her eyes, then turned and ran back into the house. Matt saw her meet Ts'ai at the door and draw her back inside.

He should be leaning against the wall instead of the shotgun. A pungent smell picked at his nose, and he tried to identify it. Kerosene! It hit him suddenly. He should recognize it; he had smelled enough of it tonight.

He moved along the side of the house, and the smell grew

180

stronger. He could see the glistening of the moisture as it trickled down the wall. He kicked the container, lying before him, and it rattled as it rolled and bounced. A new surge of anger swept away the weariness. Lo Yen had stopped Holden just before he touched a match to this kerosene-soaked wall.

He heard Holly's voice and hurried back to her. Now she had every right to know.

He opened his arms, and she ran into them. For a moment, her face was buried in his chest, then she lifted it. "What was it, Matt?" She read his face, and a premonition warned her. "Something terrible has happened."

"Yes," he said soberly. "Holden was here. He had the wall soaked with kerosene. Lo Yen came up in time to stop him from setting fire to it."

He wished he didn't have to tell her more, but his face couldn't lie for him, for she gasped, "He killed Lo Yen?"

He nodded. "I killed Holden, Holly." He wasn't asking for forgiveness from anybody, and he didn't want it.

She came back into his arms again, and he patted the back of her head. She cried hard, for he could feel the shaking of her body.

They had sat up until dawn lightened the sky, and Matt had finally prevailed upon Holly to see that Ts'ai went to bed. "You do the same thing," he insisted.

He knew how tired he felt, and Ts'ai probably had more right to it than he did. "She can tell us later what she wants done with Lo Yen."

Despite the weariness in her face Holly's eyes had been shining. She came to him, and her kiss was a fleeting one, though it carried all the promise in the world. "You know, I think I might be able to fall in love with you."

He traced her cheek with a forefinger. "I just might work on that."

"You won't be gone long?"

He shook his head. Imler insisted upon going with him. They walked down to the business district, and a wisp of smoke still trailed into the sky. Matt was surprised at the number of people on the street. With last night behind them, he had expected most of them to be in sodden sleep. He nodded or spoke to those he passed, and very few looked directly at him. Their eyes were red-rimmed and bleary, but more than just physical weariness was behind it. They had an exhaustion of the spirit, and that was more draining than the first.

Matt and Imler stopped at the head of the business district. The strengthening sun outlined the desolation with cruel light. Better than half of one block, on the north side, was burned down or blasted apart. The remaining stores on that side had had their glass shattered. Matt saw more faint wisps of smoke. Some of the debris was still hot.

The street was cluttered, and men picked their way through it. Some of them hunted aimlessly in the wreckage in hopes of discovering something salvageable. If the town wasn't dead, it was dying. Matt didn't see enough spirit remaining to even start the momentous job of rebuilding.

"Is it worth it?" Imler asked.

Matt knew the doubts that assailed Imler; he felt the same thing. How could a start be made? After last night there was bound to be hatred left, and this savage blow had wiped out a lot of the merchants' resources. "I don't know how we're going to pull them together—" His voice trailed away.

"I do," Imler said calmly. "Are you going to bring that water into town?"

Matt's weariness was a false temptress. It almost lured him into saying, what's the use, then his jaw hardened. "I'll bring it in."

Imler chuckled. "I thought you'd say that. As a start I know what will give this town a good kick in the ass. What do men need most to rebuild?" He answered his own question. "Money. I'll loan it to them on long terms. And no man will be shut out of a job because of the color of his skin."

It took a long moment for Imler's words to penetrate

Matt's head, then his eyes began to shine. All a town needed was a will strong enough and able enough to put a little money in men's hands.

He raised his voice and called to the men on the street. "Over here. Everybody! I've got something you'll want to hear."

"What are you going to tell them, Matt?"

Matt laughed in joyous resurgence of spirit. "Not me. You. Just what you told me. I can't think of a better time, can you?"

Imler watched the men coming toward him. It might be imagination, but he thought there was more vigor in their steps.

"None better, Matt," he said.